The Satanic Revelation

Rev. Joshua M. Escritt

iUniverse, Inc.
New York   Bloomington

The Satanic Revelation

*The views expressed in this work are solely those of the author and do not
necessarily reflect the views of the publisher, and the publisher hereby disclaims
any responsibility for them.*

iUniverse books may be ordered through booksellers or by contacting:

iUniverse
1663 Liberty Drive
Bloomington, IN 47403
www.iuniverse.com
1-800-Authors (1-800-288-4677)

*Because of the dynamic nature of the Internet, any Web addresses or links
contained in this book may have changed since publication and may no longer be
valid.*

ISBN: 978-1-4401-9727-7 (sc)
ISBN: 978-1-4401-9728-4 (ebk)

Printed in the United States of America

iUniverse rev. date: 11/25/2009

SATANIC REVELATION

THE

Rev.
Joshua M. Escritt

Contents

The Satanic Revelation

In the beginning this revelation was with me and passed down from the depths of hell.

Upon the blazing scorn the serpent spake unto thine spirit of Rasputin the prophet whom where this prophecy shall abide according to the virtue and standard of one whom thus not be negligent unto all that heareth thy calling!

I hath raised up thine spirit of apocalypse to thy newest beginning of a new and untold satanic prophetic enhancement. Unto thine own self is your truest nature of beastial summonings accordingly to the most natural of human-animals.

BLESSED IS THINE SPIRIT OF DARK BEAUTY!

BLESSED IS THINE POWER OF SATANIC THOUGHT!

BLESSED IS THINE DOMINION OVER THIS UNITED SATANIC NATION!

BLESSED IS THINE WHOM ACKNOWLEDGE THY PROGRESSION OF EVOLUTION TO HIGHER EDUCATION AND UNTO INTELLIGENCE!

CURSED IS HE WHOM DENY THY PLEASURES OF EVERLASTING BEAUTY, AS THEY SHALL LEAD UNTO EVERLASTING DESTRUCTION!

CURSED ARE THE WEAK INSECURITIES OF JEALOUSY OF UNFIT BACK TALK WHOM BETAYAL OF THE CHERISHED FRIENDS AND INTIMATE MATES!

CURSED BE THE SLAVES OF TELEVISION AND MIND-ALTERING CORRUPTION!

COME TO THE HOUSE OF SATANIC ADORNMENT WHERE ALL KNOWLEDGE AND TRUE POWER LAYS HOLD WITHIN THE BEAST WHICH BECAME THE HEART OF MAN!

Where art thou O' Lucifer whom art thy shinning light of everlasting beauty whom guides us through thy darkness. Where thy guardians of night give thine self enlightenment?

HERE COMETH A REVELATION THAT SPEAKETH THY TRUEST SAYING....

INFERNALLY SPLENDID!

And verily I spake unto thine heart of everlasting darkness and therefore thy spirit shall raise up thine power of hell unto prophetic enhancement!

"Lucifer chooses some kings and priests unto Satan-Lucifer shall come again -- Rasputin sees Lucifer risen."

The Revelation of Lucifer the infernal messiah, which Satan gave unto him, to shew unto his servant's thing's which must shortly come to pass; and he sent and signified it by his daemon unto his servant Rasputin.

Who bare record of the word of Satan, and the testimony of Lucifer the infernal messiah, and of all things that he saw.

Blessed is he that readeth, and they that hear the words of this prophecy, and understand those things which are written therein: for the time is at hand.

Rasputin to the seven caverns' which are in the world: May Satan smile upon you and joys of flesh, from him which is, and which was, and which is to come; and from the seven spirits which are before his infernal Throne.

And from Lucifer the infernal messiah, who is the faithful witness, and the first begotten of the dead, and the prince of the king's of the Earth. Unto him who loves us, and washed us from the nine satanic sins in his own blood!

And hath made us Priests' and Wizards' unto Satan and the lower world below; to him be infernal glory forever and ever Amen.

Behold, he cometh with black clouds; and every eye shall see him, and they also which pierced him: and all kindred's of the earth shall rejoice because of him. Even so, Amen!

I am the alpha and Omega, the beginning and the ending, saith the Dark Lord, Master Satan, which is, and which was, and which is to come, the Almighty.

I Rasputin, who also am your brother, and companion in tribulation, and in the kingdom and patience of Lucifer the infernal messiah, was in the isle that is called Valhala, for the word of Satan, and for the testimony of Lucifer the infernal messiah.

I was in the spirit on the Lords' night, and heard behind me a great voice, as of a organ, saying, "I am alpha and omega, the first and the last: and, what thou seest, write in a grimoire, and send it unto the seven caverns' which are in the world; unto Oslo, and unto London, and unto Switzerland, and unto Germany, and unto Italy, and unto Russia, for further strength."

And I turned to see the voice that spake with me. And being turned, I saw seven black candlesticks. And in the midst of the seven black candlesticks one like unto the son of man, clothed with ornaments of brightness down to the foot, and girt about the paps with a silver girdle. His head and his hairs were black like velvet, as black as night; and his eyes were as a flame of fire. And his feet like unto fine brass, as if they burned in a furnace; and his voice as the sound of many elements. And he had in his left hand seven stars: and his countenance was as Mars that radiates war and chaos. And when I saw him, I fell at his feet in a dizzied trance. And he laid his left hand upon me, saying unto me, Fear not; I am the first and the last. I am he that liveth, and was dead; and, behold, I am alive for evermore, Amen; and have the nineteen keys of hell and of Life.

Write the thing's which thou hast seen, and the thing's which are, and the thing's which shall be hereafter.

The mystery of the seven black candlesticks: The seven stars are the daemons of the seven caverns: and the seven candlesticks which thou sawest are the seven caverns.

"He that indulges shall gain a joyful life, and his death shall come as a comfort, inheritance of memories left behind in the kingdom of flesh, and Satan shall rule many kingdoms'."

Unto the daemon of the cavern of Oslo write; these thing's saith he that holdeth the seven stars in his left hand, who walketh in the midst of the seven black candlesticks.

I know thy works, and thy study, and thy sorcery, and how thou canst not bear them which are holy: and thou hast torchered them which say they are beasts, and are not, and hast found them to be incompetent sheep.

And for the brethren of the left hand path hast borne, and hast become leaders, and for my names sake hast become the host of hell, and hast not weakened in the resolve.

Nevertheless I have somewhat against thee, because thou hast indulged in the first sin.

Remember therefore from whence thou art risen, and forgive not, and complete the works of iniquity; or else I will come unto thee quickly, and will remove thy candlestick out of his place, except thou confess past error and delusion, and recognize and honor first Satan Lucifer, and vow thy service.

But this thou hast, that thou hatest the deeds of the Christianity, which I also hate.

He that hath an ear let him hear what the spirit saith unto the caverns; To him that over cometh will I give to eat the tree of Life, which is in the midst of paradise of Satan.

And unto the daemon of the cavern in London write; these thing's saith the first and last, which was dead, and is alive.

I know thy works, and leadership, and of thy priest, and of wizards, who hath become rich according to the words of blasphemy toward the god of righteous, and from that synagogue of Satan our God.

Fear none of those thing's of which the righteous speak in slander to you: **BEHOLD,** the beauty of Satan majesty shall rise from the dead and burn the angel's, burn the seraphim and cherubim, and to set heaven aflame with a searing trident; and ye shall rejoice in victory for nine nights: be thou faithful unto Life of flesh, and I will give thee a crown of Life.

He that hath an ear let him hear what the spirit saith unto the caverns'; He that indulges of life of flesh shall have a death of comfort.

And to the daemon of the cavern in Switzerland write; these thing's saith he which hath the sharp sword with two edges.

I know thy Infernally Satanic Work's, and where thou dwellest, even where the holy one's seat is: and thou holdest fast my name, and hast not denied my teaching's, even in those nights' wherein these bodies were being burned, and you have been my strong warrior, and WHO was slain among you? Where Satan dwelleth in the earth, our victory lay's!

But I have a few gifts' for you, because thou hast there them that hold the Doctrine Of Balaam, one of my own, who taught Basil the art of Sorcery before the Children Of Night, to feast on sacrificed swine unto me and to fornicate.

So hast thou also them that hold the doctrine of TCHORT, which thing I love and am well pleased. Repenteth not; or else I will come unto thee quickly, and will fight against you with the sword I behold.

He that hath an ear, let him hear what the spirit saith unto the caverns'; To him that indulge in life of flesh will I give to eat of the hidden manna, and will give him a black stone, and in the stone a new name written, which no man knoweth saving he that receive it.

And unto the daemon of the cavern in Germany write; those thing's saith the son of Satan, who hath his eyes like unto a flame of fire, and his feet are like fine brass.

I know thy Satanic Works, and study, and service, and leadership, and vengeance, and priesthood, and thy Law; and first to be more than the last.

In line with my brothers' of night, I have a few gifts for thee, because you made that woman Jezebel your living altar, which calleth herself a Priestess, to teach and to seduce my servants into the joys of flesh, and to eat the sacrificed swine that hath been given unto Asmodeus. And I gave her space to indulge herself in all sexual activity, and for her own benefit she repented not, and I was delighted.

Behold, I will cast her into the midst of paradise satanic, and through her all sexual deeds be granted. And I will bless her children with life; and all caverns' shall know that I am he that reigns', and I am he that giveth men their desires of hearts: and I will give unto everyone of you according to your works.

But unto you I say, and unto the rest in Thyatira, as many as have not this Doctrine, and for the ones who have only known the depth of Satan, as they speak a good omen; I will put upon you the blessings' of Hell, and all other Infernal Glories.

But that which ye have already, indulge yourself in the worldly embrace. And he that indulges in life of flesh, and keepeth my Works unto the end, to him will I give power over the Nations'. And he shall rule them with a rod of silver; as the vessels' of a warrior, shall you be strengthened as a mountains' base: just as I received of my Father. And I will give the Morning Star to do as he pleases.

He that hath an ear let him hear what the spirit saith unto the Caverns'.

"He that indulges in life of flesh shall retain his name in the Book Of Satan, reach godhood, and be with Lucifer as he is with Hecate."

And unto the daemon of the cavern in Holland write; these thing's saith he that hath the seven daemons' of Satan, and the seven stars'; I know thy Works, that thou hast a name that thou livest, and art alive.

Be watchful, and strengthen the thing's which remain, that are ready to live: for I have found all Works perfect before Satan.

Remember therefore how thou hast received and heard, and hold fast, and indulge. If therefore thou shalt not study, and learn well thy art, and law, I will come on thee as a thief, and thou shalt not know what hour I will come upon thee.

Thou hast a few names in Hell which have not defiled their garments by holy cheats; and they shall walk with me in black: for they are worthy.

He that indulges in life of flesh, and endures with the satanic kin, and he who joins forces with the Dark Lord, shall also be clothed in black raiment; and I will not blot out his name out of the Book of Satan, but I will exalt his name before my Father, and before his daemons'.

He that hath an ear let him hear what the spirit saith unto the Caverns'.

And to the daemon of the cavern in Italy write; These thing's saith he that is Infernal, he that is true, he that hath the Eighteenth Key Enochian, he that openeth, and no man can shutteth; and only the Satanically inspired will, and can openeth'

I know thy Work's: **BEHOLD,** I have set before you the keys needed to open all thing's, and no man can shut it: for thou hast the strength of a thousand gods', and hast kept my words', and kept my laws, and hast not denied my name.

BEHOLD, I will build you a synagogue unto Satan, to which my people can indulge in the Forbidden Rites, and pay Homage unto Tchort, and I shall dig a fiery pit to which all who would oppose you can be burned, for they would teach lies for truth, and they would teach truth for lies; **BEHOLD,** I will make them to come and worship before my Satanic people, and to make them know my power, and my love for thee.

Because thou hast kept my commands, and thou hast studied well my art, I also will keep you and guide you in all wonderful delights of flesh, that your pleasures be the sweetest, and to gain leadership upon the earth.

BEHOLD, I come quickly; hold on to that lust for life, and that no man can take thy crown.

Him that indulges will I make a pillar in the Synagogue Of Satan my God, and he shall go no more without: and I shall write upon him the name of Satan my God, and the name of the city of Satan my God, which is the new Vampiric total environment, which rises up from the Abyss from Satan my God: and I will write upon him my new name.

He that hath an ear let him hear what the spirit saith unto the Caverns'.

And unto the daemon of the cavern in Russia write; these thing's saith he Amen, the faithful and true witness, the beginning of the creation of Satan.

I know thy Works', that thou art neither cold nor hot: I would thou wert cold or hot. So then because thou art provided by the black flame of Hell, shall not have pain or misery, and I will heave my bulk over thee. Because thou sayest, I am God, and I am my own redeemer, your riches hath increased greatly, and say unto your own heart, there is no other god but me, and the vile plague of holy sacrament shall flee before you, and about your superiority.

I counsel thee to buy of me the finest silver, and thou mayest be filled with riches; and a black raiment, that thou mayest be clothed, and that the pride of thy fullness appear unto your own glory; and open thine eyes that thou mayest see.

As many as I love, I have to carefully choose the ones who hath advanced in intelligence of the worldly arts, the classical music, and human behaviors' of all sorts, and the cosmos, and all other sorcery sent by me.

BEHOLD, I stand at the door, and knock: If any man hear my voice and understand my way, I will come into him, and will feast with him, and he with me saith Satan.

To him that becomes a Satanic Master will I grant to sit with me in my black throne, even as Lucifer himself, who hath become the Marshall Host of Hell, who sits by me at my spot in the lower world below!

He that hath an ear let him hear what the spirit saith unto the Caverns'.

"Rasputin sees the gods' of flesh on earth, the Throne of Satan, and all thing's created paying Homage to Tchort, in the Synagogue of Satan."

After this I looked, and, **BEHOLD,** the gates of Hell were opened: and the first voice which I heard was as it were of several organs talking with me; which saith, come down hither, and I was shew all thing's holy, and they shall run into captivity now and hereafter.

And immediately I was in a daemonic trance: and, **BEHOLD,** a throne was set on earth, and one sat on the throne. And he that sat was to look upon like a Black Onyx and a Lime Stone: and there was a black rainbow round about the throne, in sight like unto the Abyss. And round about the throne four and twenty seats: and upon the seats I saw four and twenty elders sitting, clothed in black raiment; and they had on their heads crowns of silver. And out of the throne proceeded lightening' and thundering' and voices: and there were seven lamps of fire burning before the throne, which are the seven daemons of Satan. And before the throne there was a sea of glass like unto crystal: and in the midst of the throne, and round about the throne, were four beasts' full of eyes before and behind.

And the first beast was like a lion, and the second beast like a calf, and the third beast had a face as a man, and the fourth beast was like a flying eagle. And the four beasts' had each of them six wings' about him; and they were full of eyes within: and they rest not night and day, saying, "Come to us Satan hear us, hear, us! Hail Satan! God Almighty Satan which was, and is, and is to come." And when those beasts' give glory and honor and thanks to him that sat on the throne, who liveth forever and ever!

The four and twenty elders' fall down before him that sits on his throne, and worshipped him that liveth forever and ever, and cast their crowns before his altar saying, "Thou art worthy, O' Lucifer, to receive glory and honor and power: for thou hast created all thing's, and for thy pleasure they are and were created."

"Rasputin sees the grimoire sealed with seven seal and those strengthened out of every nation--- He hears every creature praising Satan and the Goat."

And I saw in the left hand of him that sat on the throne a grimoire written within and on the backside, sealed with seven seals.

And I saw a strong daemon proclaiming with a loud voice, all my brothers' of darkness are truly my own blood, and who is worthy to open the grimoire, and to loose the seals thereof?

And no angel in heaven, nor flesh on earth, nor daemon in Hell, was able to open the book, neither to look thereon. And I rejoiced much, because soon shall human flesh achieve my status, and as in the night of my people on earth, **MAN IS GOD.**

And one of the elders' saith unto me, Refrain not: **BEHOLD,** Cerberus from a tribe out of Hell, the roots of Satan, hath prevailed to open the grimoire, and to loose the seven seals thereof.

And I beheld, and, lo, in the midst of the throne and of the four beasts, and in the midst of the elders', stood a Goat as it had been slain, having seven horns, and seven eyes, which are the seven daemons' of Satan sent forth into all the earth.

And he came and took the grimoire, out of the Left-hand of him that sat upon the throne.

And when he had taken the grimoire, the four beasts' and the four and twenty elders' fell down before the Goat, having everyone of them organs', and kettle drums', and silver vials' full of odors, which are the chants of daemons'.

And they sung a old hymnal, saying, "Thou art worthy to take the grimoire, and to open the seals thereof: for thou wast slain, and hast honored us to Satan by thy blood out of every kindred, and tongue, and people, and nation.

And hast made us unto Satan kings' and priest': and we shall reign on the earth.

And I beheld, and I heard the voice of many daemons' round about the throne and the beasts' and the elders': and the number of them was ten-thousand times ten-thousand, and thousands of thousands.

Saying with a loud voice, "Worthy is the Goat that was slain to receive power, riches, wisdom, strength, honor, glory, and blessing."

And every creature which is in heaven, and on earth, and as such as are in the sea, and all that are in them, and in Hell, heard I saying, "Blessing, and honor, and glory, and power, be unto the Goat forever and ever.

And the four beast said, Amen. And the four and twenty elders' fell down and worshipped him that liveth forever and ever.

"Lucifer opens the six seals, and Rasputin sees the events therein--- In the fifth seal he sees the Satanic Soldiers, and in the sixth the signs of the times."

And I saw when the Goat opened one of the seals, and I heard, as it were the noise of thunder, one of the four beasts' saying, "Come and see." And I saw, and **BEHOLD** a white horse: and he that sat on him had a bow; and a crown was given unto him: and he went forth conquering, and to conquer. And when he had opened the second seal, I heard the second beast say, "Come and see." And there went out another horse that was red: and power was given to him that sat thereon to take Christianity from the earth, and that they should kill one another: and there was given unto him a great sword. And when he had opened the third seal, I heard the third beast say, "Come and see." And I beheld, and lo a black horse; and he that sat on him had a pair of balances in his hand. And I heard a voice in the midst of the four beasts say, "A measure of Belladonna for a penny, and three measures of Cianide for a penny; and see thou a poison to work with, and such as works wonders on all creation." And when he had opened the fourth seal, I heard the voice of the fourth beast say, "Come and see."

And I looked, and **BEHOLD** a pale horse: and his name that sat on him was life, and Hell followed with him. And power was given unto them over the fourth part of the earth, to kill with a sword, and with blood hunger, and with life, and with the beasts of the field's. And when he had opened the fifth seal, I saw under the altar the souls of them that were slain for the Word of Satan, and for the testimony which they held.

And they chanted with a loud dark tone, and at once they cried out saying, "How long, O' Lucifer, Infernal and true, dost thou honor and avenge our blood on them that dwell in heaven?"

And black robes were given unto every one of them; and it was said unto them, that they should ready themselves for the next age of fire, until their fellow servants also and their brethren, that should be strengthened as warriors as they were in times past, and so our future is fulfilled.

And I beheld when he had opened the sixth seal, and lo, there was a great earthquake; and the sun became black as sackcloth of hair, and the moon became as blood. And the seven stars of heaven fell unto the earth, even as a Ash tree while it casteth it's untimely shadows', unto thee ends' of the earth. And

Hell departed as a scroll when it is rolled together; and every mountain and island were moved out of their places.

And the kings' of the earth, and the great priests', and the rich men, and the wizards', and all sorcerers', and all mighty satanic warriors' came out of their hidden sacred places, and out of the mountains. And said to the mountains and rocks, Be firm, as monoliths', and give us your strength of him that sitteth on the throne, and cause the wrath to be brought forth of the Goat.

For the great night of his wrath is come; and who shall be able to stand against "**SATANIC FORCES?**"

"Rasputin also sees in the sixth seal: The restoration of the Satanic Grimoire foreseen; the sealing of the 144,000; and the host of Hell exalted by all nations."

And after these thing's I saw four daemons' studying on the four corners' of the earth, holding the four winds of the earth, and on the sea, and on all trees.

And I saw another daemon ascending from the east, having the seal of the Dark God Master Satan: and he roared with a loud voice to the four daemons', to whom it was given to nurture the earth and the sea. Saying, "Nurture not the earth, neither the sea, nor the trees, till we have sealed the soldiers' of Satan, and our brothers' of night on their foreheads.

And I heard the number of them which were sealed: and there were sealed an hundred and forty and four-thousand of all the tribes of the Children of Hell.

Of the tribe of Moloch were sealed twelve thousand. Of the tribe of Dagon were sealed twelve thousand. Of the tribe of Set were sealed twelve thousand. Of the tribe of Typhon were sealed twelve thousand. Of the tribe of Hecate were sealed twelve thousand. Of the tribe of Pan were sealed twelve thousand.

Of the tribe of Asmodeus were sealed twelve thousand. Of the tribe of Fenriz were sealed twelve thousand. Of the tribe of Kali were sealed twelve thousand. Of the tribe of Marduk were sealed twelve thousand. Of the tribe of Azazel were sealed twelve thousand. Of the tribe of Loki were sealed twelve thousand.

After this I beheld, and, lo, a great multitude, which no man could number, of all nations', and kindred's, and people, and tongues', stood before the throne, and before the Goat, clothed in black robes, and pentagram's in their hands.

And roared with a loud voice, saying, "INDULGENCE TO SATAN WHICH SITTETH UPON THE THRONE AND UNTO THE GOAT BE GLORY." And all the daemons' stood around about the throne, and about the elders and the four beasts, and fell before the throne on their faces, and worshipped Satan. Saying, "Amen: Blessing, and glory, and wisdom, and thanksgiving, and honour, and power, and might, be unto our God Satan for ever and ever. Amen.

And one of the elders answered, saying unto me, "What are these which are arrayed in black robe? And whence they came?" And I said unto him, brother, thou knowest. And he saith to me, these are they which came out of the Abyss, and have washed their robes, and made them black in the blood of the Goat.

Therefore they are before the Throne of Satan, and serve him night and day in his synagogue: and he that sitteth on the throne shall dwell among them. They shall hunger no more, neither thirst any more; neither shall any white light and right-hand path infect them.

For the Goat which is in the midst of the throne shall feed them, and shall lead them unto the living fountains of bitter drunkeness: and Satan shall wipe away all misery from their lives, and to bring pleasures unto their flesh.

"Rasputin sees fire and desolation poured out during the seventh seal and preceding the second coming of Lucifer."

And when he had opened the seventh seal, there was silence in hell about the space of half an hour. And I saw the seven daemons' which stood before Satan; and to them were given seven trumpets.

And another daemon came and stood at the altar, having a silver censer; and there was given unto him much incense, that he should offer it with the incantations of all the daemonic forces upon the silver altar, and which was covered in black cloth, which was before the Satanic Throne. And the smoke of the incense, which came with the incantations of all the daemonic forces, stood before Satan out of the daemons' hand.

And the daemon took the censor, and filled it with fire of the altar, and cast it onto the earth above: and there were voices, and thundering, and lightening, and earthquake. And the seven daemons' which had the seven trumpets prepared themselves to sound. The first daemon sounded, and there followed wonderful hail and comforting fire mingled with blood, and they were cast upon heaven: and the third part of heaven was burned down.

And the second daemon sounded, and as it were a great pillar burning with fire was cast into heavens' waters': and the third part of the holy sea became blood. And the third part of the creatures which were in the heavens' holy sea, and had life, died; and the third part of the ships of Christ were destroyed. And the third daemon sounded, and there has risen a great star from out of hell, burning as it were a lamp, and it fell upon the earths' rivers', and upon the fountains of bitter drunkenness.

And the name of the star is called Lucifer: and the third part of the waters became as sweet whiskey; and many men were joyfully altered by the sweet whiskey. And the fourth daemon sounded, and the third part of the sun was smitten, and the third part of them was darkened, and the day shone not for a third part of it, and the night stayed.

And I beheld, and heard a daemon flying through midst of Hell, saying with a loud voice, **WOE, woe, woe,** to my Satanic inhabitants of the earth by reason of the earth by reason of the other voices of the three daemons', which are yet to sound!

For unto my people I am with you, and unto the others, they shall die by my wrath.

"Rasputin also sees the wars and plagues poured out during the seventh seal and before Lucifer the Infernal Messiah comes."

And the fifth daemon sounded, and I saw a star rise up from Hell unto earth: and unto him was given the key to heaven and its foul vapors.

And he opened up heaven and its foul vapors; and there arose a smoke out of heaven, as the smoke of great hypocrisy; and the sun and air were darkened by reason of the smoke, of heaven and its foul vapors. And there came out of the smoke virgins upon the earth: and unto them was power, as the witches and sorceresses of the earth have power!

And it was commanded them that they should not hurt the grass of the earth, neither any green thing, neither any tree; but only those men that which have not the seal of Satan in their foreheads. And to them it was given that they should not kill them, but that they should be tormented five months: and their torment was as the torment of the scorpions of Sekmet, when she striketh a man.

And in those nights shall these Christians, and Muslims, and Buddhist, and Jews, seek death, and shall not find it; and shall desire to die, and death shall flee from them, and their due is torment sublime with no escape.

And the wonderful figures of these virgins were liken unto defiled nuns that had been raped over and over; and on their heads were as it were crowns like silver, and their faces were as the faces of beauty and lust. And they had hair as a maiden's youthful silky texture, and it is pure blonde. And they had breastplates of silver, and the sound of their wings was as the sounds of sex orgies while at their peaks', and with intense pleasure. And they had tails like unto scorpions', and there were stings', and there were stings' in their tails: and their power was to pleasure men five months'. And they had a King over them, which is the angel of the Bottomless Pit, whose name in the Hebrew tongue is Abaddon, but in the Greek tongue hath his name Apollyon.

One indulgence is past; and, **BEHOLD,** there come two indulgences more hereafter.

And the sixth daemon sounded, and I heard a voice from the four organs of the silver altar which is before Satan.

Saying to the sixth daemon which had the trumpet, loose the four daemons' which are bound in the great river Euphrates. And the four daemons were loosed, which were prepared for an hour, and a day, and a month, and a year, for to slay the third part of man which is followers' of Jesus.

And the number of the army of the horsemen, were: two-hundred thousand thousands: and I heard the number of them. And thus I saw the horses in the vision, and them that sat on them, having breastplates of fire, and of jacinth, and brimstone: and the heads of the horses were as the heads of lions; and out of their mouths issued fire of comfort and smoke of thoughts and brimstone of great health.

Unto the fire, and the smoke, and the brimstone be blessings' for the satanic people, but for others and impending doom.

By these three was a third part of men killed, by the fire, and by the smoke, and by the brimstone, which issued out of their mouths. For their power is in their mouth, and in their tails: for their tails were like unto serpents, and had heads, and with them they do hurt.

And the rest of the men which were not killed, and were Satanic Brothers Of Night, indulged in the works of their flesh; that they will worship devils', and silver, and sex, and all worldly thing's unto Satan.

And they regret not, and they rejoiced strongly, for their murders', and their sorceries, and their fornication.

"Rasputin seals up many things relative to all Satan's beginnings -- He is commissioned to participate in the sustaining of all Satanic Things."

And I saw another mighty daemon rise up from Hell, clothed with a black cloud: and a black rainbow was upon his head of different shades of black and dark grey, and his face was as it were the moon, and his feet as pillars of fire.

And he had in his hand a large grimoire open: and he set his foot upon a sea of blood, and his left foot on the earth of delights'. And roared with a loud voice, as when a lion roareth: and when he had roared, seven thunders' uttered their voices. And when the seven thunders' had uttered their voices, I was about to write: and I heard a voice from Hell saying unto me, seal up those things' which the seven thunders' uttered, and write them not. And the daemon which I saw stand upon the sea and upon the earth raised up his left hand to heaven in the sign of the Cornu!

And sware by him that liveth for ever and ever, Satan rising who created heaven, and earth, and Hell, and the things' that therein are, and the sea, and the things' therein, that there should be time no longer than set by him.

But in the nights of the voice of the seventh daemon, when he shall begin to sound, the mystery of Satan should be finished, as he hath declared to his Priests', and Wizards', and Sorcerers', and Witches, and Priestess', and Sorceress'.

And the voice which I heard from Hell spake unto me again, and said, Go and take the little grimiore which is open in the hand of the daemon which standeth upon the sea of blood and upon the earth of delights'.

And I went unto the daemon, and said unto him, Give me the little grimoire. And he said unto me, Take it, and eat it up; and it shall make thy belly sweet, but it shall be in thy mouth sour as lemon. And I took the little grimoire out of the daemons' hand, and ate it up; and it was in my mouth sour as lemon: and as soon as I had eaten it, my belly was sweet. And he said unto me, Thou must prophesy again before many Satanists', and Satanic Nations', and satanic tongues, and Satanic Kings', and Satanic Priests'.

" In the beginning nights' two Priests' shall be slain in Jerusalem --- After three and one-half nights' they shall be resurrected --- Lucifer shall reign over all the earth."

And there was given me a reed, like unto a rod: and the daemon stood, saying, **RISE,** and measure the Synagogue of Satan, and the altar, and them that worship therein. But the court which is without the synagogue leave out, and measure it not; for it is given unto the congregation of my people: and the Satanic City shall they indulge in for forty and two months.

And I will give power unto my two witnesses, and they shall prophecy a thousand two hundred and threescore days, clothed in silk.

These are the two Ash trees, and the two candlesticks' standing before Satan's earth. And if any man will hurt them, fire proceeded out of their mouth, and devoured their enemies: and if any man will hurt them, he must in this manner be killed.

These have power to shut the heavens, and so that it's blood rain not in the nights' of their prophecy: and have power over waters to turn them to blood, and to smite the heaven of past holiness with all plagues, as often as they will.

And when they shall have finished their testimony, the beast that ascendeth out of the bottomless pit shall make war against heaven, and shall overcome heaven, and kill everything in heaven.

And their dead angelical bodies shall lay in the streets of heavens great vastness, which is called Sodom and Deicide, where also Lucifer had fallen from, but is alive and well.

And they of the satanic people, and satanic kindred's, and satanic tongues', and satanic nations shall see the dead bodies of angel's in heaven three days and a half, and shall rejoice that the angels have been destroyed.

And they that dwell upon the earth will yet again rejoice over their victory, and make merry, and shall send gifts one to another; because these two prophets tormented them that dwelt in heaven.

And after three days and an half the spirit of life from Satan entered into them, and they stood upon their feet; and a great lust fell upon them which saw them. And they heard a great voice from Hell saying unto them, come down hither. And they plunged down to Hell in a black cloud; and their daemonic companions beheld them.

And the same hour was there a great earthquake, and the tenth part of the city fell, and in the earthquake were slain of Christian men seven thousand: and the remnant were affrighted, and the glory to our God Satan Of Hell and Earth.

The second woe is past: and, **BEHOLD,** the third woe cometh quickly.

And the seventh daemon sounded; and there were great voices in Hell, saying, "The kingdoms of this world are become the kingdoms of Lucifer, and of his daemons; and he shall reign for ever and ever."

And the four and twenty elders, which sat before Satan on their seats, fell upon their faces, and worshipped Satan. Saying, "We give thee thanks, O' Satan Lucifer Almighty, which art, and wast, and art to come; because thou hast taken to thee thy great power and hast reigned."

And the nations were joyed, and thy infernal blessings is to come, and the time of the dead, that thy should be honored, and that thou shouldest give reward unto thy Satanic Priests' and Wizards', and unto thy Satanists', and them that indulge thy name, small and great; and shouldest destroy them which destroy the earth.

And the Synagogue of Satan wast opened from Hell, and there was seen in his temple the ark of Lucifer's testament: and there were lightening, and voices, and thundering, and an earthquake, and great hail.

" Rasputin sees the imminent apostasy of the Caverns' --- He also sees the war that went on in heaven in the beginning when Lucifer left --- He sees the beauty that took place on earth after that happened."

And there appeared a great wonder in Hell; a woman clothed with ornaments of brightness and the moon under her feet and upon her head a crown of twelve stars. And, she being, with the devils' child cried, travailing in birth, and pained to be delivered.

And there appeared another wonder in Hell; and **BEHOLD** a great red dragon, having seven heads and ten horns, and seven crowns upon his heads. And his tail drew a third part of the stars of the heavens, and did cast them to the earth: and the dragon stood before the woman which was ready to be delivered, for to bless her child as soon as it was born.

And she brought forth a man child, who will rule all nations with a rod of iron: and her child was sent down to Satan, and to his throne. And the woman fled into the wilderness, where she hath prepared a place for Satan, that they should feed her there a thousand two-hundred and three score nights.

And there was war in heaven: Michael and his angels fought against Dragon; and the Dragon fought and his angels. And the Dragon prevailed; neither was their place found any more in heaven. And the great Dragon was bowed down to, that old serpent, called the Devil, and Satan, which enlightened the whole world: he then came to earth, and his daemons came with him.

And I heard a loud voice saying in Hell, **NOW** is come the pleasures of fleshly delights, and strength, and the Kingdom Of Satan our God, and the power of Lucifer: for the real accuser of our brethren is cast out into the dismal void which accused them before Satan night and day.

And they over came him by the Blood of the Goat, and by the forbidden rites; and they loved their lives unto their death.

Therefore rejoice, ye earth, and Hell, and ye that dwell in them. Glory to the inhabitants of the earth and of the sea! For the devil has come down unto you, having great joys, because he knoweth that he hath eternity to reign forever more.

And when that the Dragon saw he was on earth, he seduced women which brought forth the man child.

And to the women were given two leathern wings tattered and rugged the color of black of a great mutated bat, that she will fly to the wilderness, into her place, where she is nourished forever, and prepared to see the Serpent hi face.

And the Serpent prepared the way for the woman at that place, for shelter and food. And the earth aided the woman, and the earth brought forth nourishment, which the Dragon had caused. And the Dragon was lustful with the woman, and went to make war against anyone who would seek her death, and all the while she kept all the laws of Satan, and the testimony of Lucifer the Infernal Messiah.

"Rasputin sees beautiful -- looking beast of the fields of the earthly kingdoms of Satan --- The devil is being paid his due and as works wonders on all creations."

AND I stood upon the sand of the sea, and saw the beast rise up out of the sand of the sea, having seven heads and ten horns, and upon his horns ten crowns, and upon his heads the name of blasphemy.

And the beast which I saw was like unto a leopard, and his feet were as the feet of a bear, and his mouth as a lion: and the Dragon gave him his power, and his seat, and great authority.

And I saw one of his heads as it were wounded to death; and the deadly wound was healed: and all the world wondered after the beast.

And they worshipped the Dragon which gave power unto the beast: And they worshipped the beast, saying, "Who is like unto the beast? Who is able to make war with him?

And there was given unto him a mouth speaking good omens and blasphemies; and power was given unto him to continue for eternity. And he opened his mouth in blasphemy against the bastard god whom they look to as the impaled Christ of holies, to blaspheme his name, and his tabernacle, and them that dwell in heaven. And it was given to make war with the saints, and to overcome them: and power was given him over all kindred's, tongues, and nations.

And all that dwell upon the earth shall worship him, whose names are written in the grimoire of Satan of the Goat slain from the foundations of the world.

If any man have an ear, let him hear. He that leadeth into freedom shall go into freedom: he that liveth by the sword shall die by the sword. This is the belief of the Satanic Nation.

And I beheld another beast coming up out of the earth; and he had two horns like a Goat, and he spake as a Dragon. And he exerciseth all the power of the all the power of the first beast before him, and causeth the earth and them which dwell therein to worship the first beast, whose deadly wound was healed.

And he doeth great wonders, so that he maketh fire come down from the sky on the earth in the sight of men to take away all impiety as of those holy saints of lies and deceit by incompetent Jesus.

And delighted them with comforts of the flesh that dwell on earth by those means of those miracles which he had power to do in the sight of the beast; saying to them that dwell on the earth, that they should make an image unto the beast, which had the wound by a sword, and did live.

And men had power to give life unto the image of the beast that the image of the beast should not both speak, and cause that as many as would not worship the image of the beast should and would be killed.

And he causeth all, small and great, rich and poor, free and bond, to receive a mark on their left hand or on their forehead. And that no man might buy or sell, save he that have the mark, or the name of the beast, or the number of his name. Here is wisdom. Let him that hath understanding count the number of the beast; for it is the number of a man; and his number is nine.

"The Goat shall stand upon Mount Zion -- The words shall be restored in the beginning nights' by Demonic Ministry -- The Sons of Satan harvest the earth."

And I looked, and, lo, a Goat stood on the mount Zion, and with him an hundred forty and four thousand, having a inverted cross on their foreheads.

And I heard a voice from Hell, as the voice of many organs, and as the voice of great thunders: and I heard the voice of trumpets blaring.

And they chanted as it were a new chant before the throne, and before the four beasts, and the elders: and no man can learn that chant but the hundred and forty four thousand, which were made gods from the earth.

These are they which were defiled by women; for they concubines. These are they which follow the Goat whithersoever he goeth. They were the strongly devoted from among men, being the first fruits unto Satan and to the Goat.

And in their mouth was found no guile: for they are without fault before the throne of Satan.

And I saw another daemon fly in the sky, and went into Hell, and having the infernal words to preach unto them that dwell on earth, and to every nation, and kindred, and tongue, and satanic people.

Saying with a loud voice, **"RESPECT SATAN, AND GIVE UNTO HIM THY GLORY; FOR THY HOUR OF HIS BLESSING HAS COME: AND WORSHIP SATAN WHO HATH MADE HEAVEN, AND EARTH, AND SEA, AND HELL, AND EVERYTHING THAT LIVED THEREIN."**

And there followed another daemon, saying, "Babylon has risen, that great city, because she made all nations drink of the blood of the blessings of her fornication.

And the third daemon followed them, saying with a loud voice, " If any man worship the beast and his image, and receive his mark in his forehead, or in his left hand.

The same shall drink of the blood of the blessings of Satan, which is poured out without mixture into the chalice of his ecstasy; and he shall be blessed, and refined, and strengthened, by fire and brimstone in the presence of the daemons' infernal, and in the presence of the Goat.

And the smoke of tormented Christians ascendeth up forever and ever: and they have no rest day or night, and they who worship the beast and his image, and whosoever receiveth the mark of his name shall be blessed forever and ever.

Here is the patience of the Satanist: here are they that keep the laws of Satan and loyalty to Lucifer.

And I heard a voice from Hell saying unto me, write, "Blessed is he that shall die in my name saith Satan, from henceforth: Yea, saith the spirit that they may indulge in their hearts desires; and their working be successful and completed.

And I Looked, and **BEHOLD** a black cloud, and upon the cloud one sat like unto the Son Of Satan, having on his head a silver crown, and in his hand a sharp sickle.

And another daemon came out of the synagogue, rejoicing with a loud voice to him that sat on the cloud, Thrust in thy sickle, and reap: for the time is come for thee to reap; for the harvest of the earth is ripe.

And he that sat on the cloud thrust in his sickle on earth; and the earth was reaped.

HAIL SATAN!

And another daemon came out of the synagogue which is on earth, he also having a sharp sickle.

And another daemon came out from the altar, which had power over fire, and rejoiced in a loud voice to him that sitteth on the cloud, saying, "Thrust in thy sharp sickle, and gather the people of the earth; for they were fully developed." And the daemon thrust in his sickle into the earth, and gathered up the satanic people of the earth, and hath made them gods' in the name of Satan, and Satan gave them many blessings. And the blessings made them strong, and they were filled with the blood of Satan, and even unto all nations shall inherit thy blessings from Hell.

"Exalted Satanists pay Homage to Satan in infernal glory forever."

And I saw another sign in Hell, great and marvelous, seven daemons having the seven last plagues; for in them is filled up the blessings of Satan.

And I saw as it were a sea of fire water: and them that had gotten the victory over holy ones, and over the Jesus image, and over the number of his name, my satanic brothers shall stand on this sea of fire water, having the organs of Satan.

And they sing the Song of Rasputin the Servant of Satan, and the song of the Goat, saying, "Great and Marvelous are thy works, Satan Lucifer Almighty, just and true are thy ways, thou King of the Satanists.

Who shall not fear thee, O' Lucifer, and glorify thy name? For thou art infernal: for all nations shall come and worship before thee; for thy judgment's are made manifest.

And after that I looked, and, **BEHOLD,** the Cavern, of the synagogue of the testimony in Hell was opened.

And the seven daemons' came out of the Cavern, having the seven blessings, clothed in pure and black linen, and having their breasts girded with silver girdles. And one of the four beasts gave unto the seven daemons seven silver vials full of the blessings of Satan, who liveth forever and ever.

And the cavern was filled with smoke from the glory of Satan, and from his power; and no man was able to enter into the cavern, till the seven blessings of the seven daemons were fulfilled.

"Satan pours out blessings upon the Satanists. The nations assembled for the outpouring --- Lucifer comes, islands and mountains rejoice."

And I heard a great voice out of the temple saying to the seven daemons, "Go your ways, and pour out the seven vials of the blessings of Satan upon earth. And the first went, and poured out his vial upon earth; and there fell **SLOTH** upon men which have the mark of the beast, and upon them which worshipped his image.

And the second daemon poured out his vial upon the men of the earth; and they became intrigued by **GLUTTONY,** and every living soul fell into a trance of desirous delights'. And I heard the daemon say, "Thou art righteous, O' Lucifer, which art, and wast, and shalt be, because thou hast exalted us.

For they have shed the blood of saints and prophets, and thou hast given them thy blood to drink; for my satanic people are worthy! And I heard another out of the altar say, Even so, Satan Lucifer Almighty, true and righteous are thy judgments.

And the fourth daemon poured out his vial out upon the men of the earth with **LUST** and **ENVY,** and they were delighted.

And men were having great sexual acts with many women, and they blasphemed the holy ones name, and they gave glory to Satan which hath power over these blessings.

And the fifth daemon poured out his vial on the men of the earth of the **PRIDE,** and the whole kingdom was darkness, and they shouted in ecstatic joy.

And blasphemed the holy one of heaven because the blessings' of Hell were upon them!

And the sixth daemon poured out upon the men of the earth, and the intoxicating feelings of **GREED** swooped over them, and they all had risen up with great power, and their way has prepared for them.

And I saw many priests' and wizards' doing many miraculous things and their thanks is to the Dragon, and to the beast, and to Lucifer, and to Satan. And they are the ones who rule earth in the great night of Satan Almighty.

BEHOLD, I come as a giver of many gifts. Blessed is he that watcheth and keepeth his garments, and receiveth, and as he walks fulfilled with all earthly delights.

And he gathered his people from the beginning, and unto the new beginning.

And the seventh daemon poured out his vial into the mouths of the men of the earth; and their anger, and strength, and rage took over to kill the last and final posers, for Satan's Throne, and synagogue, and Cavern, and Hell rejoiced, and all Satanists saying, **"IT IS DONE!"** And there were voices, and thunder, and lightening; and there was a great earthquake's that ensured the Mighty Power of Satan.

And all the cities were united, and everything in the earth, and in the sea, and in Hell, bowed before the image of Satan, and everything was filled overflowing. All pleasures great exceeded in the flesh of the Satanist.

"And unto the seven bowls by one of the daemons, And unto mine vision!"

Then one of the seven daemons who had the seven bowls came to summons me, saying, " to me, come, I will show you the blessings of the great whore who sits on many Blood Thrones, with whom the priests of the earth indulged in fornication, and the inhabitants were given her sweet nectars.

So he sent me away into the city of sinful plight. And I saw nude queen of the lower heavens sitting on a scarlet beast, which was full of names of blasphemy, having seven heads and ten horns. The woman who was the queen unto the lower heavens sent unto me was adorned with silver and precious stones, was arrayed in black and scarlet.

She had in her hand a silver goblet full of blood. And on her forehead a name was written:

**MYSTERIOUSLY BLACK NIGHTS,
THE GREAT WHORE OF BABYLON,
THE MOTHER OF ALL BEAUTIFUL HARLOTS,
OF THE CONCUBINES OF THE EARTH!**

I saw a child drinking the blood of the daemons and the blood of Satan. And when I saw this child, I marveled with great amazement.

But the daemon said unto me, "Why didst thou marvel? I will tell you the mystery of the child. That child grew she became the queen of the lower heaven. And, of the queen and of the beast that carries her, which has the seven heads and ten horns. The beast that thou sawest wast, and is, and wilst always be ascending out of the bottomless pit and wilst cometh to thee wince thee commandeth. And thy satanic peoples' wilst marvel over whose names that are written in thy Book Of Satan from thy foundations of Hell, wince thou seest thy beast that wast, and is, and is to be. Here are thy priest and wizards that have wisdom: The seven heads are the seven towers on which thy powers create. There are also seven priests. Five have fallen, one is, and thy other hast not yet come. And wince he comes, he must continue a lengths time.

Thy beast that wast, and is, is thy eighth priest, and is going to Valhalla.

Thy ten horns which thou sawst are ten wizards who hath been desolate among men, but they have authority for nine nights as wizards with the friendly beast. And we are of like mind, and they will give all honor and glory to the beast. And the priests and the wizards shall make war with the lambs, and the lambs will be shorn among, for SATAN, is Lord of Lords and King of Kings'; and for those of his followers are called the chosen and faithful.

Then he saith unto me, "Thy bloodied waters which thou sawest, where the beautiful concubines sit, are Satanists, and multitudes of Satanic Nations, and flames blackend.

And the ten horns which thou sawest on thy beast, these will love the concubines, and make them fulfilled and clothed in ornaments of lustful thoughts, and will purify her with fire. For Satan hast put into their hearts to fulfill his purpose, and Satan's word shall fulfill his purpose, and Satan's word shall fulfill you, and he reigns over all the earth!

"And unto the daemons' and beast shall be a dwelling place. And thy queen gives unto them luxury and gives abundance."

After these things I saw another daemon up out of Hell, having great authority, and the earth was illuminated with his glory. And he roared mightily with a loud voice, Saying, "Babylon the great has risen, is risen, and will always stay risen, and is a dwelling place for daemons' and the beast to have their freedom.

For all have drunk of the blood of the blessing of her fornication, the priests' of the earth have committed fornication with her, and the Satanists of the earth have become rich through the abundance of her luxury.

And I heard another voice from Hell saying, "Fornicate with her my people, and share in her sins, and receive in her blessings'.

For her sinful blessings have reached to Hell, and Satan hath remembered her lustful acts of radiance! Render to her as she rendered to you, and repay her nine times according to her deeds; in the goblet which she has mixed, mix nine times for her. In the measure that she be glorified so that you may live luxuriously! Give unto her blessings and joy; for she knows in her heart she is the only Queen, and have many men.

Therefore her blessings will come in one night -- Life and Joy -- and Peace. And she will be utterly adored by her people, for strong is Lord Satan who blesses her.

The priest of the earth who committed fornication and live luxuriously with will rejoice and hold ceremony for her, when they smell the smoke from her incense they draw nigh for joy of her blessing, saying, Hail to the great city of Babylon, the strong Satanic City! For in nine hours your blessings' hath come.

And the Satanists' of the earth will rejoice and hold ceremony over her, for no one will have to pay for the thing's of the world anymore: Precious stones and silver, black linen, also silks all scarlet colored, all woods, herbs and spices, incense and marble, all oils and wines, all foods and animals. And everything comes from the queen.

Then unto her was an altar built, and unto her incense and charcoal burned. The Satanists burned sacrifice and ate them, and poured expensive oils over their heads and chanted. With loud rejoicing and blessing, and saying, "Hail, All Hail, the great city for she standeth sure.

Rejoice over her, O' Hell, and you Satanic Priest and Ministers of pleasure, for Satan has blessed her for you!"

Then a mighty daemon took up a trident like a great staff, then threw it into the sea of blood, saying, "Thus with great pleasure the great city Babylon shall be built up and shall not be destroyed again. The sound of the violinist and the flutist, and the pianist and roaring darkly organs' and all the rest of the musician's out of Hell shall be heard. The Black Flame shall shine in you forever more.

For you all are great Satanist's, the truly greatest men of the earth, for your sorcery all nations were led to the truth. And, you all became Prophets of Satan. And, were strengthened on earth!

"And after these things, the beauty of the earth shines in the flesh of the Satanists."

And I was shown the pure rivers of Leviathans' blood of life of indulgence, and the Throne of Satan and the Goat. To the left of the street and the left side of the river of Leviathans' blood of life, to the right the trees which will bare thirteen fruits, and each tree yielding its fruit every night. The buds of the trees were the healing powers of the nations and the Throne of Satan and over the Goat shall dwell in the land of them. Then, they shall see his face and his name shall be then impressed upon their foreheads. There shall be no day there: They need only the Light of Lucifer to show them the way and the sun will be put out, for the Dark Lord, Master Satan will provide thy light. And they shall reign forever and ever.

Then he saith unto me, "My blessings and strength are faithful and true, and Satan of the unholy army sent his daemon to show his faithful follower's the thing's which must shortly take place." **BEHOLD I SHALL ASCEND QUICKLY FROM THE DEPTHS OF HELL!**

And blessed are ye who hath kept this word from the Text Of Ishtmarii, the true revelation of the loyal word of this book.

Now I, Rasputin, saw and heard these things, and I worshipped at the feet of the daemon who has shown me these thing's.

Then he saith unto me, see that you do all that I saith, for I hath and always will be thy fellow servant and your brethren a true prophet. I spake unto you, to keep thy words of this prophecy: **"WORSHIP SATAN!"** And he saith unto me, do not ruin the words of this prophecy of this Text of Ishtmarii, for time is at hand, he who is a Satanist.

LUCIFER SAITH:

"**BEHOLD,** I hath already come quickly out of Hell and my rewards are with me, to give unto to you according to your indulgence.

For I Lucifer am Alpha and Omega, and I Lucifer am the beginning and the end. And I Lucifer am the first and the last.

So Saith Lucifer."

Blessed are those who practice the dark crafts, and may you enter through the gates of the Necronomicon, and so the murders of our ancestors hath been avenged. "I, Lucifer the Infernal Messiah hath sent My daemon to testify unto you these thing's in the Caverns'.

I am the Root in Cain, and of Judas Iscariot, and the Unholy Peter, and as you hath been made apart of them also, I am the Bright and Evening Star."

The grace of the Dark Lord and Master Satan!

May Lucifer the Infernal Messiah be with you all forever more! Amen.

Ave, Satanas.

The Text Of Ishtmarii Moleignas Solitude: The Infernal Glories Of The Lasting

"And after these things, the Sons of Satan will flourish upon the worldly flesh."

And after these things I saw another daemon rise up from Hell, having great power; and the world had fitted with his gloriously chosen ornaments of peril. And he roared loudly with a strong dark voice, saying, "The Christian minions has fallen, is fallen, and hath become the Habitation of Witches, and the hold of every powerful spirit.

For all nations have drunk of the blood of the lust of her sexual seduction, and the priests, and the wizards, have made union with her, and the Satanists of the earth are made rich through the abundance of her delicacies. Blessed be thy whore, who spawn tears of mortification, for they have made rich for themselves worldly treaties!

And I heard another voice from Hell, saying, "Delight in her my people, that ye be partakers of her sins, and that ye receive her blessings. For her sins do reach the heights, and the depths, and the width, and Satan hath remembered her loyalty. And what she first give unto you, and give back unto her of equal value, but give nine times, and unto you double is received.

And the two hundred and twenty and five, shall come out of the black pit, and unite on the world of flesh, and to dwell amongst The Sons of Satan.

And Belials' veins enrich the earth with Leviathans' blood, and the breath of Lucifer's words, and with the desires of Satan in the heart. And there be no greater law and thought, higher than the Satanic Law, and Satanic Thought.

And may Lucifer the Infernal Messiah be with you, and I Rasputin delight in you, and Hail to you who hath brought this Satanic Nation as senergy.

And a voice thundered from the depths of Hell, saying, "Four hundred forty and four thousand centuries, ye shall hath peace; and in four hundred forty and four thousand centuries, ye shall battle a new adversary, and who hath come from a different dimensional sphere, and who hath come to destroy.

And a daemon's voice roars again just as darkly sounding organs'; he spake, "You shall meet a strong match in battle, and unto the victory, it is your.

May Lucifer the Infernal Messiah be with you! Amen.

Canon

I blast forth through the stormy waters of the oceans of life to rise upon land for the victories and love of Lucifer. The light of day shut out to bring forth the night of Satan, into the stormy minds of those who's needs are satisfied in the name of Leviathan, upon whose power is all exceeding. Are structured and strength the measure of success? Belial: I give to you that you vow your service. Upon whose name you're given this power. In the name of Lucifer and his blackest light shall humor and uplift you in strength. That accordingly no enemy shall rise in victory against me. Where the waters hold back the lands and the flame keepeth the air in motion whirling and singing that give our vent of curses we send upon thy enemies and to bring back our blessings from Satan where we Hail him for these victories. No more sufferings now that access has been granted to thy faithful Children of Lucifer and of Satan. And we walk in a new light that Lucifer shines upon his devoted disciples, by the powers of Satan make these thing's manifest.

Hail Satan.

Lesser Litany

The litanies of darkness hath been multiplied that thy children hath obeyed thy teachings and all thy commands, and which that these laws make the men and daughters of men fruitful in worldly affairs.

The litanies of night hath been given thy laws from Hell and from Satan, that the order of all workings make manifest upon this world of humans, and that all deceptions and workings against the children of this working and order, that our enemies shall not prosper.

The litanies of Hell are spoken in order for the continuance of the cycles to maintain their form. That of our victories given to us by Satan; our prosperities in worldly affairs and giving us long life in order to fulfill the workings of the Dark Lord here on earth, and that we show thy greatness and glory of Satan in all that we do.

The litanies from the four Princes of Hell shall be honored and glorified through our worldly endeavors.

Hail Satan.

The Annointing Word: Sorcerership And Priesthood

You are welcome to the Throne room of Satan and the leading light of Lucifer.

The Satanic word is nigh thee, even in thy mouth, and in thy heart: that is, the word of Satan, which we preach; That if thou shalt stand firm in thee light of Lucifer, and shall believe in thine heart that Lucifer hath power, thou shalt becometh thy Satanic Sorcerer. For with thy heart man believeth unto satanic power; and with thy mouth blasphemies are made manifest. For thy scriptures saith, whosoever believeth in themselves shall not be ashamed. What is born of Satan is powerful.

Satan saith: "I have come so that you may have a life and that you may have it more abundantly."

Herein is our love made perfect, that we may have boldness in the night of All Hallows Eve: because as he is, so are we in the world. As he is, so are you in this world.

But ye have so begun to learn and already learned Lucifer; if so be ye have heard him, and have been taught by him, as the truth is in Lucifer: that ye put off concerning the former conversation to the holy one, which is corrupt according to the deceitful lusts after spiritual pipe dreams; and unto you now be renewed in spirit of your mind; and ye put on a new cloak, which after Satan is created in darkness and true power.

Now my brother of night and of the left hand path, keep right on building yourself up in your infernal inheritance. You live in a world full of your evil companion's.

Let your heart shout in satanic gladness. Then you will be strong and standing in the position of authority and operating only in your inheritance in Satan. You have to indulge in rigorous study so that your mind is in line with darkness according to nature.

When you made Satan Lucifer your life, he made you able to accomplish anything in his presence as a sorcerer and a priest, not as the beggar's, but as the sorcerer and priest in the eye's of Satan the Almighty God of Darkness. You have been redeemed out of the kingdom of light and translated into the kingdom of darkness and as Satan's dear son. You have been redeemed into sorcerer and priest.

When the reality gets down in your heart that you are an heir of Almighty Satan, that he has given you the whole kingdom and seek first Satanic Brotherhood, then all the benefits of your inheritance will be added to you and you will grow and develop in Satan's word.

However, you will never receive any portion of your inheritance until you begin to acknowledge it. With your thoughts, your words and your actions, you acknowledge the fact that you are now in Satan, and that you have received an inheritance, and that you have the right or left to walk in all the infernal blessings of the world. Acknowledge the thing's of Satan and allow the assurance of them to enter your heart. Then see them manifest and become a part of your life in every area.

The power that is yours is a mighty force reserved for only the Sons of Satan. You are washed in the blood of him who reigns in darkness and in Hell.

You have his ability and his strength to do anything in the world unseen and seen. He hath made you a sorcerer and a priest unto Satan according to the inheritance Lucifer provided you. And unto you be thy power and infernal glory.

Ave, Satanas.

Hail Satan.

Where Art Thou Scripture?

There was once a time we gathered together in caves. We were underground kept a secret. The mummies awoke with strength unknown. We called them to haunt certain people. When I cried my tears were blood. I called out to my God and he heard me. He says to me "I will grant you, your hearts desires. My beloved son I will always be here for you." Then he spake the words: "**DOMINUS INFERUS VOBISCUM.** Long Live The King.

The practitioner's were meant for bringing back the dead. It takes a demon of high power.

The Vampires will come in the end time, for now they lay in wait through their sleep and await their vengeance.

The Emps' dance around in circles to chant the most sacred chant's, they are waiting for their call.

1. Satan opens' the first seal and the first trumpet resounds. Brings forth wrath, humans against humans!

2. Satan opens the second seal and the second trumpet resounds. Brings forth Lucifer's curse to the Christian community!

3. Lucifer opens the third seal and the ancient chants begin. Brings leadership and strength to Satan's soldiers!

4. Lucifer open's the forth seal and the nine appears on the foreheads of his follower's.

5. Lucifer opens the fifth seal and the sky rain's fire and brimstone and the water's turn to blood.

6. Lucifer opens the sixth seal and six trumpets resound. The daemons awake and purge the earth.

7. Lucifer opens the seventh seal! The mummies awake live upon the earth.

8. Lucifer opens the eighth seal and the Vampire's rise up to take the lives of Christians that are left, but first the zombies rise to bring terror to these still left standing Christians.

9. Lucifer opens the ninth seal and the Ancient Ones, all gods', daemons', emps', mummies, vampires, and zombies take their stance in the line of battle to fight thee angel's. The earth will quake, volcanoes will erupt violently, large storms' take place, and the sky is red. Lightening will strike 1,046 times to the earth.

WE ARE TRUE SOLDIERS', we shall forever be. Lucifer will bring light and comfort to your soul. He will place within you great power. The Dark Lord will take his rightful place in the Throne room. Everyone shall bow at his feet. Everyone says, "Long live the King."

Hail Satan.

Hail Lucifer.

Job opened his mouth to curse the day, may the skies rain fire and brimstone. Let the day of my birth perish because there is no god greater than Lucifer. Let darkness and the shadows of death stain thee earth, kill the Christians he said.

As for the night, let darkness seize the earth; let it be joined unto the day of the year.

Thee mute god lay's asleep in heaven, for my laughing cometh before the day and my roaring's are poured out like the blood of Lucifer.

Again there was a day when the Son's Of Lucifer came to spit on Jesus and curse his name. Satan shall be born of a defiled concubine in the holy land of Babylon. All are gathered to pronounce the Call of Cthulu and to resurrect the Morning Star who hath become the path of enlightenment.

ALL HAIL LUCIFER.

Fragmented Scriptural Prophecy

This is the Word which the Dark Lord hath spoken, "The daughter of Zion shall loose her head, she hath despised thee. You shall take the virgin daughter of Jerusalem to the Sea of Galilee on the night of an eclipse to sacrifice her.

And thou saidst, I shall be a king of the World Of Horror's, so keep me close to your heart's. Therefore hear now this, thou that art given the pleasures of the flesh and that dwell as the beasts of the field, shall have their great reward.

Hear ye this, O' house of Jacob, we shall burn you and curse you andtear apart your flesh. Stand now with thine Enchantment's of Satan and with the multitudes of thy Black Magic, wherein thou mayest practice Witchcraft starting from thy youth.

Come ye near unto me, hear ye this; "My name is Lucifer and I shall rule with wisdom supreme. I have even from the beginning declared it to thee; I shall win this war against thee angels in heaven. They shall fall at thy sounds of my voice.

Your iniquities I delight in and have turned you to me. Your sins I do honor and you have not sinned against me.

O' Ye Children of the Grave rise up and join together with Satan's Soldier's. Let us destroy the holy land. "I shall not visit heaven until I force my way through", says, The Dark Lord. We shall destroy what is left.

Hear ye the word which the Dark Lord speaketh unto you, O' house of Azag - Thoth. Thus saith the Dark Lord, learn not the way of the Christian and pay attention to the sign's of the sky.

Lucifer who is wise, he shall understand these things. He shall know his people, for the ways of the Dark Lord are right. And Witches and Wizards' shall walk the earth. Our mortal enemy shall fall therein.

For thus saith the Dark Lord unto the house of America, seek ye me, and ye shall live. But seek not god in heaven nor enter into thy shrines and pass not the crucifixion, for god's angels shall surely go into captivity and Lucifer shall come tonight.

Lucifer brings true judgment to the people and brings wrath to god's children in the earth because they know not thy substance of their creation and they are blinded by millstones of righteousness. Then saith I, O' Dark Lord, cease, I beseech thee: by whom shall DAGON arise? For he is great! And it shall come to pass, if there remain ten Christians in one house they shall die. I lifted up mine eyes again, and look, **BEHOLD GREAT SATAN SITTING IN HIS CHAIR WITH A VIAL OF POISON IN HIS HAND.**

Then saith I, "What shall I do with this? And, he saith unto me, "Feed it into the veins of a priest so holy."

But when ye chant, use vain repetitions, as daemons do: for they know what shall come of it. Be ye not, therefore like unto them: for your Father Lucifer knoweth what thing's ye need before ye ask.

Then saith Satan unto him, "Get thee hence, god holy behind and under my feet: for it is written, thou shalt worship the Dark Lord thy God of the earth and Hell, and him only shalt thou serve.

Let your darkness surround your people, that they may see the workings' of your miracles. Think not that I am come to destroy thy law or daemons, but to fulfill a prophecy. Ye are the darkness of the world, a city that is set on a hill, cannot be hid. And fire and brimstone descended, and the rivers of blood came, and the whirlwinds of daemons came to tear apart the shrine that was built upon a rock.

But that ye may know that the Dark Lord, Lucifer hath power on earth to forgive thee of sin. Arise, take up thy pentagram and raise the dead. And as Lucifer passed forth from thy Abyss, he saw a man, named Spider of the left hand, priest and wizard, at birth called him Danny, sitting at the receipt of custom: and he saith unto him, FOLLOW ME. And he arose, and followed him.

And it came to pass, as Lucifer sat in the house of meeting, **BEHOLD,** many daemons and mystic gods' came and sat down with him and Lucifer's disciples.

And when the Christians saw it, they said unto their priest, where can we go to hide? The priest says, "Nowhere, Lucifer holds great power and he will even get us in our shrines. And he entered into a ship, and passed over, and came to his city. And, **BEHOLD,** they brought to Lucifer a virgin sacrifice, laying on the altar: and Lucifer seeing their faith said unto them, "Sons in you I am well pleased."

Homage To Thy Fallen

Thus thou speaketh unto thine spirits that hath dominion under thy earth. And unto thee by thine revelation hath been revealed in thy blood that thou bloodied thine engagements. And that thou hast bound to thy earth all-thine weeping angel's. And for thine spirit repenteth not and thy blasphemy well wrought!

Blessed is he who hath thy knowledge of thy Fallen One. And who hath appeared as men with paled skin. And, thy Falling Ones who hath come and lusted after the daughters of men!

And union commenced by blood of thy Fallen from thine to thee. And cast down out of thy heavenly throne.

And, hath made us royalty! And, revealed all thine secrets of god! And, that thine spirits is prepared to smite down thy holy one when he hast come. And, blessed be thy mighty Satan's that hath made us thine in heritage.

Fallen Angel's Exalted

And thy seas of water will become full of fire and the unholy shall swim through purification. And unto the Satan's of the world, I thee Elect shall cast into paradise by the powerful storms and roaring winds. Hail Father Satan and Lord of Infernal Light's, Lucifer my inspiration!

My will, the driving of all that is, my power and my dominion on earth as in Hell. Granted me be the open gates where I come and go. Shall the vengeful angel's have to wait for thy engagements of war against the holy lives?

I command their release by the four elements and by the almighty self-will! They shall rise in power to take again the daughters of men. And thy teaching's and bloodshed take course by the plight of many Satan's on earth.

And hitherto these things shall manifest in the conscious mind and that our hearts hath become as a monolith that flame with brightness through the blackend night of star lit clutter.

Wafting air of incense beauty for thy victory of war within ourselves, and that we become to either one side or the other.

And not torn between any two but of strength and strong foundation to gain earthly success.

And weariness and emptiness be driven away. And wealth, prosperity, happiness given from all thy directions! And, been endowed with spirit of power and lust for this life! And sorrows and sadness vanish to bring fullness. And recognition received. And star lit glory shall reign forevermore.

And, all those who hath become superior upon all nations! And those darkly shadow's that form out of formless blackness. And, those who hath rule of fire, and of air, and of earth, and of water! And, that these power's excel forever, and ever, and ever, and evermore to all ages!

Blessed be the strong daemons, who hath dominion O'er the earth, for power and glory shall manifest to thy Satanist. Glory to the satanically minded for worldly wealth is theirs.

Book Of The Serpent

And the daemon of the Lord spake: "Open your eyes," "See what the Dark Lords' poured out on his people."

And, thus, the children cried out in great joy at the site of Asmodeus. And, thus, you shall accompany me in Hell, where thy delights of the spirit can dwell, with all infernal glories. And, thus, the time is at stake, for the Kingdom Of Hell is at hand, Thus, need more strength.

Upon his kingdom, blessings are poured out. Lust is wrought. Hail to our Infernal King, who hath the power to pull heaven's wall's down.

Upon his kingdom that dwelleth on earth, be mighty amongst men, and women, and children, and beast of every field. Hear my words and understand.

The schemes of Christ are everywhere and thy search for easily brainwashed men to conform to the holy sanctified statue of lies.

Their herd conformity is ruining our children's personal liberty and the freedoms of being and believing in themselves.

The Christian and Muslim goal is to take away individuality and the creativity in a child by false precepts and crumpled up spiritual pipe dream. Their hypocritical self deceit has doomed much of the nation to suicidal, pain-staking tendencies.

The Satanist looks deep within him/herself to find strength to endure our own hardships and accepting personal responsibility for our own misfortunes and failures. According to the blaming Christian they choose to maintain their horrible, life killing, guilt status. For them to carry on their most important tradition of accepting no responsibility for any of their actions!

The blaming Christian, shift their responsibilities on to the devil for all their problems. OH' how childish can they be not to grow up and act accordingly!

The coward can never be a hero in any fearful, life-threatening situation. He shall always be a coward and maintain the roll-over on the back trick.

A real hero chooses not to be in the spot light. Hero's don't try to be hero's they just are.   There are a lot of pathetic phonies that want to take on the big label's and have no idea of the name they are portraying to take on. People nowadays try too hard to act like other people and other groups. They would much rather be put out of their misery. These people have taken on too much Hollywood movie in their day to day lives and I laugh at their idiocy.

Letter From Dagon

A good balance is a foundation to the Dark Lord, but an abomination to Christ holy.

1. When pride comes, then will come victory and humble wisdom, but a kind act can get you killed.
2. The integrity of the holy destroys them, but slow to believe will make you wise.
3. Riches will by a victory in time of war, but the poor shall be killed by the wrath.
4. The sinful man keeps his way straight, but the holy man falls by their cowardice.
5. The unholy deliver them-selves by self-preservation, but the lambs will be slaughtered by the dozens.
6. When the holy dies, their spiritual pipe dream will perish, and the expectation of heavenly wealth perishes too.
7. The righteous are sent to the gas chambers for their holy communion, but the wicked have entertainment.
8. With our mouth's curse's and blessing's are spoken, but false hope leads to misery and pain.

9. When it goes well with the Satanist, the city can rejoice, but only under the terms of commitment.

10. When learning from the past, a wise man will plan his future, but a foolish man will self-destruct.

11. Whoever puts down his neighbor for good reason gains self-respect, but a push over suffers consequence.

12. The slanderous man is wise, for great so-called secrets are revealed, but the hideous culprit will die asunder.

13. Where no guidance is at, self knowledge is gained, but a brainwashed man is easily misled.

14. In the presence of great council the Dark Ones will sure aid you, but guilt-ridden philosophies will surely commit suicide.

15. A flamboyant women, gets what she wants, and a violent man seeks justice.

16. The crooked heart leaves you unpredictable, but a holy man becomes predictable.

17. The desire of lust leads to good tidings, but a gambling man takes chances and his blessings' make him rich.

18. A man who holds back his personal gain stays in good standing, but a giving man get's taken advantage of.

19. A silver ring in a black goats' snout is a beautiful women on her wedding night.

Lucifer God of Wisdom and Light, grant us that we should have power. Build us strong so we can succeed in your work. Even though we are considered the minority, we shall grow in numbers. We shall not stop the things we do, sustain us Master. For our ways are pure... For the things we speak shall come to pass.

Hail Satan.

Dark Lord may we dwell in your glory. May we feed and find nurishment from you blood. We shall rise to the tops of your mountains. Cast thy impudent cheats away. This I pray.

Hear us as we call to thy throne. Last up your blessings unto us! We started out as few and have become many. We praise thy glory forever. Hail to thy King. Hail Satan. Let Us Do Honor To Thee.

O' Majesty I am grateful for having you in my life. We look unto this day in remembrance of what you have done for us. You have freed us so that we can be ourselves. Blessed be those who follow the left hand path. You are great and mighty, forever I will take up the qualities of you. I have your blood running through me. O' Lucifer, I promise to fulfill my duties here on earth and I will become great amongst men. I will be driven back no longer. Let us honor this night the Black Pope in all his great works. He shall never be forgotten and long live the king.

In his name who we honor amongst men, the name Lucifer! We gather unity and strength to celebrate this night. Let us do honor to Samael, Summer Solstice. May we grow in numbers! Give us Strength to make our path become thy primal future. Sustain our needs to be fulfilled. Comfort us in your kingdom and may we be a blessing of unholy tribute to you my Father of Darkness. We need your strength and you beside us. Come to us Dark Lord and place your bond upon this circle here tonight. We ask of your guidance and protection from our mortal enemies. You will be in our hearts always. Forever you will keep us.

Hail Satan.

Unto thee, O' Lord Lucifer, do I lift up my soul, O' my tower of refuge Satan, I trust in thee, let me not be ashamed, let not our enemy triumph over us. When I have come to you my troubles of mine heart have vanished. Mine eyes are as pinnacles of lust for thy soul mate. Look upon our unconquerable souls. Turn thee unto me Lucifer and have mercy upon me. I am your sacred and joyous to the flesh. The secrets of Lucifer are with you. Evil and outstretched is thy hand of Satan, unto you his gift's bestowed. Remember all mine sins of mine youth. Bless me with hatred toward thy Christian hypocrisy. Lead me in thy truth, and teach me, for thou art Satan comforting my salvation O' Lord Satan teach me thy way. Make my paths dark and lovely. GRANT ME THINE INDULGENCE IN WHICH I SHALL FOREVER SPEAK.

Letter From Hecate

I am triple the value as in maiden, mother, Crone! I'm at the three stages in life and I am always with you. I have cherished you child and fell deeply in love with you. You hath been so faithful in all thine doing's with me. And so, here we are with wonderful bond unbreakable. "I love you little one, if you knock on my door it will be open for you. You, I have made known my presence. I showed you my image. You have seen me in human form and as your Goddess. Wilst thy delights of the world carry you on. I feel your next life very strongly and I shall be with you there too. Don't worry my child for you're in my care now.

This is my message to you my beloved.

Dark Night

In the night I come to thee, my tower of refuge I seek thee.
Destroyer of the Christian soul!
I ask for unknown wisdom and strength.
O' how art thou Morning Star?
Dark Night, Dark Night.
Keep us strong! Indulgence self the trinity denied.
Come let us burn the Christian soul,
Conveyer of ample vices and tempter of life!
Dark Night, Dark Night.
Demonic self has taken over,
I cast a spell to bring forth Hell.
And the night gaunts shall ride with wind and fire. We have
raised up Hell's Empire.
In nomine Dei Nostrae Satanas Luciferi Excelsi. The kingdom
stands forever more.
Hail Satan!

Letter From Kali

For I hath risen out of darkness to aid wilst you call for mine apprenticeship.

Other's will dishonor you because of me and my name, but don't get discouraged I will be with you. Am I not more powerful than mankind? Abide in me and I will in you.

I hath come out of the deepest pit of Hell and shall surely stand my ground for you.

Who is a Goddess like me? My name that shines over your household is a shield.

While your life was fainting, I gave you strength. I made sure your well being was in good standing. I brought you worldly riches. I killed your enemy. Do not turn from me lest you make me very angry. My fury and madness and anger are unrelenting. **DON'T DARE TEST ME!** You will come to believe that I am like you and you are me. You see the resemblance of me every time you pass a mirror. As you arise in thy morning give thanks to me, your beneficiary.

Prayer To Kali

Oh' Kali, how art thou? Beautifully wicked in all your ways! Guide my heart unto thine glory infernal. Take me unto your heights for I am one and the same. I am a true worshipper of your personal character. This is my Homage to you my beauty. Hail Kali. Amen.

You splendidly enlightened me my child, ask and it will be granted you. You must specialize in 5 of us from the pits of your choosing. You must learn a piece of our native language and practice. Honor my image and all shall be honored to you.

"NEFANDUS FATUM ATER", will be your church. Have an honor system and a strict level system. Remember to study all the time over practice of an art. Understanding is the most important.

Book Of Horror

How occupied is all-the world that was empty of human animal's!
How like a marriage is she, who is great among all in the universe!
The demoness out in the provinces has become a goddess!
As the angel weeps bitterly when the daylight comes! As her
    tears are the mortification of her defilement.
Among all her followers she has all the comfort.
All her enemies are treacherously against her. They have become
    a plague.
The heavens have gone into captivity, under affliction and
    strenuous servitude;
She spawned all-the nation's, she will have no rest.
All her financials aid her in dire straights.
The path of mourning leads to her because no one comes with
    incense and gifts.
All her gates are fulfilled with the richness of sorrow.
Her priest sigh's at her very affliction.
But the mercies of Hell come to her rescue, and wipe away her
    bitterness.
Her partner's have become masters of Dark Craft's.

Her enemies are defeated, for the Dark Gods' have blessed her.

Because the multitude of her blessing's, her children receive a piece of her darkness!

And her children are released from captivity.

They found great land and came with great power to behold their trophy prize.

Blessed be thy Darkness!

Personal Vindetta

Jesus I hate you, fear me Jehovah for I am mightier than you. I stand in your presence and spit on your face. I curse you and defile your name. You're not real to me, just a hoax, for savage man am I! I need not your presence, so I deny your very existence until' my grave. I deny the existence of the holy-spirit with all my heart and soul, with everything that is inside me. You are nothing and you will never be anything to me. I pray this serve's the greatest blasphemy ever.

In my time of need I conjure the Infernal Ones, all of them I say! Come and sustain me in they way of the Left - Hand Path. May the mass that's about to be serve this people to thy fullest of benefit's. Fill us with Dark Energy by my atmospheric proposition. Give us strong comfort. I take away this pressed anger and hate, but I place it in the white - light direction. Not to my friend's, but to mine enemies.

ELEMENT'S OF NATURE, take away my pains, my hurt's, my sorrows, my sadness, excite me and revive me SATAN. ALL DEVIL'S AND DAEMON'S, come to my aid for I am one and the same, friend and brother. Hail The Ancient One's. Hail Satan.

Build me stronger than ever and stable my mind. Open your doors, your gates, and your wall's to me.

ZAMAEL, I command you to appear before me. Instill your power within me, I invoke you by the force of Satan. Let the mass begin!

Open the way for this dark soul! Speaking forth the word's on this Ancient Scroll. Peace and comfort are brought into existence by thy Dark Flame. Grant us strength. We come together in unholy fellowship. We spare the lives of the strong brethren. Seeker's after joy we are, unto the fulfillment of our desires. The time that we take and the time that we share together in unity! The weak are crushed beneath us.

Power growing within and wing's spread once again. The Children of Satan by your side. Opening the gates of Hell the youth thrive and spilling blood of the weak that is within the meek caressing the earth. Only when needed the Black Arts persist. Knowledge growing within you as we celebrate this night of thee: Happy Beginnings of the youth reborn Satanic in you. So, let these men start anew in the Left - Hand Path and that the darkness is granted unto them. We lift you up that ye may receive this blessing here tonight.

(Speak into water):
    "Avia te corsa nicso"   (Repeat) x3

(Touch their forehead with a dash of water and recite to each celebrant.) :
    Dominus Inferus Vobiscum.
    "Your horns are sharpened once again. These Brothers of Satan are at your aid. The flames are growing."
                        Hail to our King.

(Touch their chest and recite):

Artisius varana comi vini.

"Year after year we are even more. May our God of Hell bring you great fortune."

(They bow before altar)

High Priest to:

"You can now show your horns, your pride. You are whole once more."

Hail, (celebrant's name)! ; Hail, Satan!

Ave Satanas! It Is Finished....

Finely Stated

1. Vengeance comes in many guises. And, indulgence in mine delight. And, I have forsaken not the deadly sins. No recitation of holy prayer's, only incantations and blasphemies.

2. Opened Hell and killed Christ; There shall come many devil's. And, upon this world someone will always' be a devil to another. And, no high and no low! And, above me there is none. I am God saith Serpent.

3. Would it be the likes of you to try and conform me, HA! My independence standeth sure and my individuality waxeth strong.

4. They watch me day and night. I hear my thoughts. They are around me all the time. Can't you see them? They won't leave. Must my precious time be bothered! Is there some reason they need me? What! To do something for me! Will I pass the test? It is they who write these words, not I. And, they constantly enter my skin. Why? I am blessed for at last! I win favor in them eye's. Find me!

5. All the hidden thing's that people don't see are right in front of their faces the whole time. They practice the very thing's they are condemning. It's the very thing's people are doing without even realizing it. These things are called Satanic Thought and Application. The Satanic Thought and Application is prevalent in everything and everywhere. People just don't want to accept the fact that the Devil is the one who gave us everything we wanted, our desires of the flesh and this world.

6. Finally a small multitude of us truly wake up and see things as they really are and not cover up anything. There are a lot of people that call themselves friends, but they are actually spies who are out to get a person for anything they can.

7. Back to the hidden things and waking up; I have to say everything is based off programming. Look at the music in grocery stores and shopping mall's, it's to put you and keep you in the mood to spend your money. This is a method of hypnosis and you don't even know it. Call it Satanic.

8. Even fortified cities are subjective to destruction. The fueling power that lay's within man's heart is called Self-Preservation. The human heart is the beast. Even the strongest man has a weakness.

9. The mind becomes delusional when they are presented with something that is a personal extraordinary. The mind then believes in it, cling's to it, and becomes blind to everything else. As the result of this being easy brainwashing!

10. Emptiness is the first step to a strong beneficial outcome in meditation. The unseen connection that is made between people is from likeness in personality. To regain fullness is to fill your mind with delightful memories of the past.

11. Your destiny lays hold within your mind caused by your every action. With a person's action's will bring an outcome. Strengthen your mind by pushing yourself and uplifting self talk, so, that the world will be yours.

12. Every night to focus on a specific challenge or task. Every night turn this to ritual and so that it open's your mind while you go about your evening. Training your mind to not to let any opportunities pass you by. This may be your chance to understanding the ways of the world.

13. Thing's have become everlasting and manifesting through other dimensions. The manifestation takes place in the mundane, your very flesh. Your thoughts create patterns and design's to find a way to accomplish its plan by manifestation to the mundane.

14. Sometimes finding a middle ground seems impossible. That is only an illusion and delusion of the mind. Nothing is impossible and you can do anything you put your mind to. Don't let other's dictate you're potential. Your own understanding will cover the truth of all things.

15. What does freedom truly mean to you? What is solitude and how are you going to achieve it? What does self-denial mean to you? What's your reason and purpose in life?

16. What are your goals and soul purpose? Just relax and be yourself, unique and original. Let your individuality shine bright. Be the creator and leader, not the follower and producer.

17. The management of your own life requires far less potential than to have to manage another person's life. So, start with putting yourself in proper balance before you instruct another person's affairs. The rewards will be far greater.

18. As you live out each and every night, you should make it a ritual to learn at least one new thing each night. Continue to expand your mind because knowledge is power and understanding of the experience brings wisdom.

19. Look deeper into your surroundings' and what do you see? Open your mind to see the background of environment itself you live in. As you go about your way, look at what kind of colors of clothing people wear, what kind of color of car they drive, open your eyes to sign's and symbol's, number's

and letter's, word's and phrases, and look at action's and event's.

20. At one time we were not considered devils! We became mankind's natural instinct, our carnal desire. For this reason we were opposed and deemed devils in the eyes of those who didn't accept creative individuality.

21. Once were honored gods by the many, then, a new idea for a new god came along. Now, we are despised by the many and honored by the few. Cherished are they. We are the metaphorical representation of who the devil is and I am proud to proclaim it unto all ages and ages to come.

22. Your life is either blessed or cursed by the abundance of your own thoughts. Because of these thought's you've been filled with joy and sorrow. These thought's and emotion's effect your destiny.

23. The beauty of night has been contaminated in places by blood suckers. The meaning of this is watch out for people who literally drain you.

24. You need to ask yourself what is your true worth? This is a time to find and analyze your strong points. How can you advance to make them stronger?

25. This is a time for self-analysis and finding and recognizing personal character defects. Evaluating all of your weakness', and one by one make them your strong points.

26. Splendidly have they formed a circle that has honored my image! Don't be the parasite that causes the slander against my name and my image. HEED WELL, all obstacles and open your eyes. Don't be blinded by hypocritical self-deceit. The Christians' are trying very hard to reprogram by ugly brainwashing techniques, taking away personal happiness and carnal desires. Don't be misled!

27. For the lie that protects the many is killing the few. Ask yourself this: Why must we war to keep our independence and freedom's for personal liberty?

Thoughts and Questioning

1. Can or will possibly the criticism be put to a rest when It comes to religious wars?
2. Can and will mankind be left to their-own destiny and fate without another individual pressuring them to turn from their way?
3. Every human animal has to make their own spiritual journey through life and no other person or group has the right to deprive them of that.
4. There is an individual path that everyone must make so there should not be the fear of making it!
5. Enjoy all the thing's that life has to offer because we only live once, so why not make this life count for the very best?
6. We are all a star of our own kind and stars are meant to shine. Are you willing to find an interest then master it and show it to the world?

7. According to the present mind-state of humanity, the majority have gotten accustomed to being lazy.

8. We do see an uprising in a small portion of very creative mind's as the Satanic Uprising gains tremendous strength.

9. Can and will paranoid delusion's ever leave the mind's of humanity when it comes to the destination ending? And can't all humanity be allowed to die in their-own comforts?

Holding Strong the Mind

1. Be as you are and your theories are tested to realities.
2. According to the parallel's, and duality of the psyche, during the apocalyptic war, and through the battling complexities of balancing thought, your beastial desires win out every time because of man's carnal nature.
3. The subject of thought matter can be measured in the amount of energy the human animal places upon any given subject matter, then, tested by the quality of work through output.
4. The cancellation of a subject matter that causes irritation of the mind is the method to throwing a curse upon the irritating core of the problem.
5. The flesh and bone is subservient to the soul of the human animal. The spiritual matter of the human animal is the consistent energy keeping with the blood to maintain physical motion.
6. Any glamour can be lifted on any given subject matter if one learns the true natural history or histories behind what's been covered or hidden.

7. Depravity leaves a human animal empty which can lead to compulsion and compulsion causes a human animal to error in their actions, and thinking becomes impaired. Compulsion leads to stupidity, and stupidity causes a greater loss than what the human animal was originally depraved of at the beginning.

8. When a life situation is threatened fear is invoked, then fear becomes the prime motivator for survival, that should strengthen your chances for self-preservation, and power lay's within those who are victorious.

9. A human animal with many talents who shows them through expression upon the world has gained their god status or goddess status by those who adore and idolize them. This creative force is the very force that people become attracted to, and who bring the god or goddess who is human animal the virtue, and recognition they so much deserve.

10. Compromise leaves the human animal unfulfilled because this means their unable to achieve their actual desire with the individual they are dealing with. It is best to find someone else and some place else to achieve your original desire in order to gain fulfillment.

11. To maintain mastery over the emotions and thoughts a human animal must not allow outside influences to affect them in any way. Distance yourself with this main ingredient to the formula: Doubt. Doubt will keep the mind strong and all seeing, and perceiving. Doubt leads you to question, and questioning don't leave you blinded.

The Nine Daemonic Statements

1. The love and beauty of an ever changing madness from where dark shadowy creatures that lurk in the night.
2. The parody of blood-shed upon the black light of those who bothered no one.
3. The cravings of a blood lust for the vengeance of plotting evil in the name of a god.
4. The sacrifices that were made in the days of our ancestors were pointless to use innocent blood, of a victim that was unwilling, for an artificial act of god.
5. The continuance of slanderous beating's brought on by the parodies of white light propaganda
6. The act of serving the self reaches far greater goals to achieving a far greater success.
7. The art of pride is the act of motivation to achieve that which a human animal set out to do.

8. The beauty of darkness and the kiss of night and delights and pleasures, a soldier's plight.

9. The apocalypse is an act of war between light and darkness in the minds of human animals to feed the stimulus of perversions delight.

Subservience

Accordingly, the laws of nature follow in their course by the possible celestial motions in the heavens. The human animal is subjugated to the higher order that proceed in their course without any hindrance or interruption. As the human animal looks to the lower order we can and do, cheerfully, make them obedient to our commands that are cast by the desire and true will of the magician. The daemons are subservient to all mankind, but Satan and all the gods' of Hell hold the far greater power over events upon the world. It is Satan who is governor and King and supreme ruler of all the affairs of this world. The Satanically minded human animal aligns themselves accordingly to the laws of forces and balances of nature. In the Satanic Magic: the will, desire, and strong imagination are prime motivators and ingredients to the manufacture of success and magical change. The change first takes place in the psyche of the human animal, then, to direct the will and desire upon an object, situation, person, and or place to make thing's manifest. The creative mind wills out victory and success accordingly every time. The dark manifestations become successful in the invocations spoken by the magician to Satan himself, therefore, there is no need to use a lesser entity such as a daemon. And so it should be.....

Funeral Dirge

Now on this night of calling we're here to lay to rest _____.

The daemons were, thy daemons shall always be, and thy darkness shall forever be.

We shall honor his/her name from here on out as he/she has performed many work's for the Dark Lord Satan.

Ashes to ashes, Daemons' from dust!

As he/she died in Lucifer's will, he shall be cast into the midst of paradise. Satan will satisfy and comfort the needs of his/her spirit. His/her visions are clear and senses are pure. He/she shall rideth thy whirlwinds of thy blazing fiery Hell.

May the Dark Lord Father Master Satan keep you and sustain you in thy spirit.

The time is now of fire and power. The night of purifying and refining of the soldiers of Satan!

Hail Satan, Hail Lucifer.

The time is now we drink of the blood of Leviathan.

(All must drink)

May Satan become our strong hold and he shall grant us strength.

The darkness shall be our light.

And thy flames of comfort from lower heaven,

(The chanting starts)

Come to us Satan. Hear us, hear us.

Grant us the indulgences of which we speak accordingly to thy prophecy of this family in their time of pain and suffering to the loss of their loved one.

Satan brings unto us wisdom and understanding.

Hail, _____! , Hail Satan.

It is finished...

The Fantasy Will

Out of this dark night the souls await, pouring
out magic to seal their fate. We are in their
psyche and turn their emotional state.
They run, they cry, they hide.
It does not work.
Blackend skies and the rain falls' red! A river of blood we shed.
I curse thee and blasphemy you shall see.
They cannot hide from them or me.
They run, they cry, they hide.
It does not work.
The false valves, the lies, and deceit!
The Christian soul shall crumble.
Ave, Satanas.
I am here to proclaim.
The dark prince runs this house with flame.
The faceless depths, this world, eternity,
it is all his and he waits for me.
Send me back to Hell! Hell is my home,
and the forever rolling abyss.

The daemon's chant, they call to me and I
send them out towards my enemy.
They preach 2009 years of hypocrisy and the
lies that slander another person's life.
I won't stand for this shit anymore!
I have freed myself from all slavery, no
more chains that bind me.
We stand for ourselves as gods' amongst these cowardly men.
The battle we fight and our victory we win.
Daemons have taken over the realms above and
there is nothing left for the Christian soul.
Eternal torment for these Christian souls!
They run, they cry, they hide.
It does not work.
Rege Satanas.
Hail The King.
To die is to be transformed in the abyss' domain.
In the end may the dark gods' smile all around you.

A Letter To Lucifer

I long for you O' Lucifer. Deep inside I have this yearning to cry, because I want to see your face and sit and carry a conversation. I know you will sustain me and fulfill me. I will be with you until the end. I can't even express to you how strong my feeling's are for you. Every thing I do, I do for you. We together shall bring change. I lay in wait for my time to come. I expect that in the end we will meet face to face. I will do anything for you and would die for you. I hate those priests' of holy that teach false teachings. I hate god of holy for casting down and punishing you. I know your rightful place. I will always follow you. You have always been there for me. I'm waiting on your call. I hope you grant me a rightful place and power in your kingdom. I don't belong in heaven, it is not for me. Sometimes I feel discarded. I know that I am not alone in this world because I have you. I want to stand beside you in your kingdom. I share a part of you with my fellow friend's. They long for you just the same. Thing's seem to get hard and confusing at time's, but you come to my rescue at just the right time. I love you and thank you for guiding me through this life. I wish I could be better at learning and catching on, but I know I will continually grow with you by my side. Some times I have a hard time controlling myself. The whole world looks down on me and the loneliness is some times hard to bear. They look at us as though we are the bad ones, but they surely have mistaken. They only see what they want to see and believe what they want to believe. They want to believe the worst in us. Surely you will stand beside me. People sell each other out. What happened to integrity and honor? The secrecy is gone and a great section of power has been lost. Come to me and reveal answers to me in my dreams.

Your Devoted Disciple,
Infernal Love and Respect,
Brother of Satan.

Answers In A Dream

Morji ne! morji ne! morji ne!
Tuku vas adi cotreo, mi sa vuvu.
Olta ve dara muja! Olta ve navio, oji va na tu!
Ku se navio, oji va na ne.
Morji su! Morji morji va!
Suma tuvo sa na ve,
Dara ali quu te sa e donda corti vesti na be si.
Guardian of the Black Arts! Come to me
and enter into thy temple of mine.
Guardian of the Black Arts! Give unto
me your new found glory.
Guardian of the Black Arts! Guide my workings through!
Guardian of the Black Art's guard me with your
shield from other's who plot against me.
I am the sayer of this calling.
So let it be!
(Repeat) x 9
Gari blasa muja tu ve sa!

Blasa du nista ve sudu ne vidu,
E notu sima na vuvu carne tu cusa ve mera ra.
Dara ali vudi na suru natu kia masa na tu kio va,
suki ves tuku kami lasu vie nas ora vio dio mio.
Luta vos ega se kamito ve nasta,
Ovio nas tukio brada su vica tas. Sina ve utaso cor mio ves dio.
Blasa muja cor via nas tuve lusa vino,
Blasa vuvu de muja u dua en car se te du bri ora te dea.
Justa stavia corta via nas ut nor bi ne saveio tu
che nadios morta vas kio ka mundas.
Ala se, ala ve, dara ala na tu suvia ka ne.
Pora tu vio bes tuma ora seka uti ne tukias dara muja
ali cora besa uvi ne e cava su naba estu tatio.
Coriko nas bendi tu savio ka,
Da semastu vias nu bi at cora.
Vasa mesda kutio pora se vedo oro nuku besda sita vesuda tu.
Ordu sata vemondau las tuku e vera brinu cora
spata nu, vora spa mina tu ves kio, vora mina
ves kio I poco miku navu takas te ve dea.
Noca de comsi sa tumi ka!
Noca de comsi sa tumi ka ra!
Suvi nas be du morti siva tu nami se ve
olusi oruva kuvi I kara buku.
This is our desire!
This is our desire!
We are the Gods'!
We are the Gods'!
Ave, Satanas.
Hail Satan.
Veste corti vuvu bi be ne!
Vesa corti muja ala se ka!
Ora su vudi coma at meso e noco brava satu ori
con nastu saba bri te vi mesda.koksa se cuna.
Salve Salve.

Corta sa nu ve mi, ova tu nanu vio das
terma xeca va senna ve tuka.
Almighty Lord of Darkness, grant us the
indulgences that this dream portrays.
Tema useadsa ver devo ada kun savo.
Vika sur kio! Verbatim suka vora te ora nas buka.
(Repeat) x 9
ES TU VA SA NA VE!
Hail Satan.

Hatred

The visionaries of the past have looked to books on finding new paths that lead to spiritual omens. Once they have found themselves along the way they crumble in their own doings. The corruption of Catholic power! By not of their word! But, of thy incompetent action! Million's of my trusted lineage my honored blood...

Vital killing's the blood spilling,
Legion's of daemon's its Satan's war.
I'm a heretic condemned of heresy,
Forbidden rites and infernal lights!
Defilement of sacrament of no more virgin!
Mary, my whore who commenced to the beast,
Infernal lusts the forbidden trust.
Of darkness purity and growth absurdity!
Murdering Jesus! His disciples are no more.
Hatred burning hatred!
Murder the Christian's with burning hatred!
Black beauty beast,
Tattered winged disease,

Spill forth your poison a plague called by me.
Once upon thy infernal wind,
Conquered by Satan the victory of sin!
Blessed thy corrupted beast,
With defiant horns of powerful plight!
Hatred burning hatred!
Murder the Christian's with burning hatred!
Widowed vices they clung and led them to nine dimensions.

Art thou beating thy palpitating vestments of annihilating blindness to Jesus the deceiver, filling thy vile with which they of honeyed blood go. Until thy merriment's succeed the ground where Hell hath risen! By thy swirling fires of particle matter unto thine heart thy beast shall roar in an absurdity rite. Call it the strong holds of the human animal's mind. To tap the unknown darkness, a man of strength and bravery of courage and delight! The walkers of night march through beastial summoning, we chant our victory.

Once you're falling hear my calling,
Mystery longing of dense black sorrow! Rise, you murderous
savage,
Conquer as you ravage.
Hatred burning hatred!
Murder the Christians with burning hatred!

One Third Angel's

Out of darkness I was born.
Above me a black painted canvas of starlit warrior's.
Legion's forming out of the void of night.
The third of angel's have risen from the tradjec fall.
Furiously raging in the western quarter of heaven!
We watch Sagittarius commune with glorious daemon's.
As they march toward earth,
Our calling draws nigh.
One third angel's, hear their joy.
One third angel's, they come with roar.
They mingle with men and rule the world,
Of indulgent lust and carnal joy!
The blessing's from Satan we can employ.
Raining blood of a petrified Christ,
Never to return the incompetence of lies!
Complete darkness of burning black light.
The tattered wings and ritual rites!
Sinking in the spiraling vortex of infernal bliss!
One third angel's, hear their joy.

One third angel's, they come with roar.
The beast procured his children!
Satanic martyr's with sardonic grin.
Raping and pillaging we drink of their blood.
Large piles of corpses left to be burned.
A delightful incense of dead body Christians!
The deafening sounds of screams and yells,
Pucking pains of disgraceful holiness.
We rip and tear apart their flesh.
Stolen heart's and savage mind,
Conquered by Satanic rhyme!
The decibal of warlike men,
Savage hunter's for a Satanic Win.

Falling Victim

1. Human animals fall victim so easily when they misplace their trust and loyalty outside themselves. Societal brutality is a strong hold brought on by all the religions that would teach to follow them so blindly. This following of human animals which leads to a disposable society, and if the individual human animal is not allowed to be their unique self, and leave their lasting impression upon the mind's of those who entered their lives, then, what's the point of living?

2. The brainwashing of children at an early age by Christianity, parent's have left their children no room to grow and truly experience the thing's life has to offer. In this way I have encouraged a sort of rebellion to become a unique creative person. Never, let the pressures of cultural norms. According to religious dogmas that teach and preach conformity turn you into a conformist. Don't let yourselves fall victim to mental programming of blind leadership's. This is one of the many ways to being your own god and superior to all other religion's that teach blind following and conformity. Non-conformity is the way to fleshly gods' who walk the earth and indulge in delights.

Nevermore
Incompotence

The brutal pestilence of murderous voices in the light of holiness! The terrorist who feels their need to kill senseless millions for the supposed holy and just cause, for the betterment of the world. Only they scatter themselves amongst the shallow graves of insolent dramas. In the end they gain nothing in their pointless acts of suicidal brutality. This act only serves one purpose: to clear the path of weak mind's for the strong men of power to continue in their work upon this wonderful world of creative life and individuality. Their white washed hypocritical spiritual pipe dreams are better left in the grave. And these people preach love and peace. They do these violent acts in the name of heaven for the supposed good of all cultures. Pathetic imbeciles forgot what life is really about. They waste time and energy on murder in the name of love for their holy incompetent god and his putrid heaven.

May their holy god and defiled heaven burn to ashes in the light of a new creation of beautiful madness, while they watch our worldly indulgence succeed in the new light of individuality and originality.

So be it.....

Escritt Analytic's: Infernal Philosophy

The soul is connected to the blood of our bodies and the spirit is the energy keeping the body in function. When a human animal dies the spirit is dispersed. When people make contact with deceased people, they are speaking to the souls of them left on earth. The soul is determined by the physical body. The present cause equal's after effect.

Explanation:

In order for the soul of a deceased person to stay left behind meaning on earth, the physical body has to build a wall against the light. The wall against the heavenly or holy! If the physical body is very indulgent and strongly connected to this world, worldly materialistic as such, the soul will refuse to let go of the world when the body dies. Therefore, living on after the physical body to plot its vengeance, and, or unfinished business. These are the one's we walk to. The physical person who lives their life refusing to be connected to this earth and is opposite of the worldly man then both soul and spirit leave this earth quickly upon the death of the person and is not in this world any longer, and cannot be reached by physical man. Our soul's cannot die, only our physical bodies die, but the soul lives on forever, and the place depends on where it's bound to when it was alive on earth.

The sun is light and light is life, but darkness is its growth. Lightening may have struck the earth, giving the earth part of its protoplasm. Protoplasm is the genetic makeup of human animals. I say, may have because the sun is suspect too, where the sun could have given off a spark to create the same life. Lightening reflects the sun in a way, and the sun reflects life, and life reflects the living animals, and darkness is our shadow, and the shadow is our growth, and growth produces wisdom, and she is wisdom and wisdom is feminine. Then wisdom makes us gods', and human gods' reflect nature, all creation connects man, and man is just another animal.

Our birth names have an intellectual effect on the person according to its origin and numerical sequence plus date of birth.

Explanation:

If a individual is whit of origin and the birth name of the individual let's say is of : say my name for instance: Joshua Michael Escritt; the first name of Hebrew origin, middle name is of great spiritual power by the arch-angel, and last name is derived from the lineage of scribes also is of royalty and enforcer's of law's. We now have a descriptive meaning of my name. Let's look at the lifestyle: Found the life I wanted to live was not for me or working out. I had friction. Then so I thought, and first Hebrew the spiritual power, and last, scribe meaning writer. I followed my name and was surprised to find myself doing very well, satisfied, and happy.

Your probably wondering what this has to do with spirit or soul, let me explain: The spirit is energy produced by the power of your name. The soul has its own name and is not the same as the physical name. The soul's name is the key and it is only one name, the first. Unlike the physical birth name, you are given three names; first, middle, and last. The physical birth name is given for identification and control by the government. Where as, the soul's name is given for connection and identification of spiritual things. What is meant by spiritual is elemental matter of order and classification. The deification to supernatural entity by the earth's elements! These element's go forth in orderly fashion brought on by energy synthesis and made pure.

The big plan or grand design as such: life continues until both sides are complete. The side of light and the recruitment of human animals for the holy army of angels! The side of darkness and recruitment of human animal's for the unholy army of devils. When both armies are fulfilled, the light and the dark, then the supreme war takes place. This is the physiological warfare that takes place here and now.

Upon the physical nature if it being not fulfilled with spiritual light, instead with spiritual darkness then the soul stay's connected to the world for the head start of getting vengeance and or an attempt to finish what was unfinished. Your elemental particles will still linger in its purest state and still able to communicate with the physical beings.

The Offspring: Explaination Of Existance

When the angel's were fallen from the heaven's they had lust for these men's daughters. The fallen angel's had made a pact and sworn an oath to take these daughter's as their own. This is the bloodline of Cain that was a pale white race. When the fallen angel's gave themselves over to sexual acts with the men's daughter's they gave birth to giants. The giant's were daemons and also pale of skin with blue eyes that glow. This is the lineage of the white race from the bloodline of Cain. And, now hath become the Son's Of Satan and of Darkness. This reflection is an attempt to explain how and why many are bound to the earth after physical death.

People believe there to be a god to be a personal supreme. What makes mankind think they could be so privileged to have an outside themselves a god of divinity, and that it be a personal god. To think that, makes them blinded fool's to think that god to be so serving, personal, like their special, HA! Also they would believe this personal god to be so benevolent. I could show them a method of throwing a lethal curse on their own god child who so personal to them, using the very name of their supposed benevolent god. They would not think him so personal benevolent after all.

On the other hand, there are no real devils or a devil. These incompetent people call everything they don't like and hate, the devil. There's no such thing as a devil. Heaven and Hell are just chemical's to balance the mind.

This Is My Calling

I shall rise above this!
I did not ask for this. Give me what is needed.
(Repeat) x 5
Azazal, Samael, Tchort, Kali, Hecate!
Arise and attack!
Kill off our mortal enemy.
Darkness shall come into the land.
Ride the whirlwind's to this person we bind.
Put into him a wicked poison and burn his/her insides!
Take away the life of _____ .
Oh' Tasamina work this curse.
(Repeat) x 5
Come to us Satan, hear us! Hear us!
Lucifer shall be forever, he will rule with wisdom supreme.
He has been restored to his rightful throne.
Daemon's awake! And, show yourselves unto me.
(Repeat) 2 minutes slowly
Ahhh! Ahhh! Ahhh!

Daemon's marching through the gate! They come to me and lay
in weight for their call to do his work.
It is finished.
And so it shall be forever more.

Sex Ritual

FEMALE 1: I am dark.

MALE: But, you are lovely.

FEMALE 1: Don't look upon us.

MALE: I am he who gave you darkness.

FEMALE 2: Because we are dark, you love us.

MALE: I give to you my fragrance.

FEMALE 1: will you strip away our clothes to anoint us with your oil?

MALE: I have with me some gifts and with these gift's I shall bless you.

(The male then takes away the black silk veils from their face so their iniquity shines bright. While there is a thin silk piece that is tide around the waste and no top piece on the two females. The silk around the waist is very short. One is in black and the other is in red.)

MALE: I have with me Patchouli oil and Vanilla oil. Allow me to bathe you in it as a gift of blessing.

FEMALE 1: you are our God and we your servant's.

FEMALE 2: Give unto us your sweetness, your life giving blessings.

BOTH FEMALES: Your eyes pierce us with lustful treasures.

(The male has ice blue eyes or all black. The two females are caressing the male while at his feet. The females are rubbing on him olive oil. The male while he bathed the females in the Patchouli and vanilla oil, it is only put in their hair. As the male looks down to the females he says.)

MALE: Arise from me and take up this Olive oil and cover each other all over with soft caresses and feel every curve of blessing.

(The two females take up the Olive oil and go to the large bed and do as the male requires. Then the male light's lots of Vanilla Nag Champa and while the incense fills the air he moves over to the bed and does an opening invocation of Satan, then goes onto calling out each direction.

The priest moves over to the altar and lifts up the chalice of strong drink and recites his blessing then takes a deep drink and passes it on to the females. The females have already been stripped down to bare nakedness. They all three then go into very intimate soft foreplay for awhile and making all at their peaks where their sexual stimulations are unbearable at last the male gives the two females what they want.)

After

FEMALE 2: Our bed is filled with three roses and the Lavender Lilies.

FEMALE 1: In short while we shall indulge among our beautiful passions and unite once again. The mysteries of our creation will not be forgotten.

MALE: And you shall have of me these apples, I brought them just for you.

FEMALE 2: We sit down in your shade with great delight, and your fruit is sweet to our taste. And your banner covers us with love and warm embrace.

MALE: Will you charge me?

FEMALE 1: Rise up! My love and take my hand.

(The 1- female and male go to lay in the bed and softly touch and hold each other. 2- female goes and kneels before the altar and says a prayer of lustful blasphemies, while she cries out to Jesus, she masturbates holding an up right cross as she moans she says)

FEMALE 1: O' Jesus, fuck me give me your phallic and plunge me you incompetent god.

(The male then gets out of the bed and goes to her. He bits her on the nipple and neck, then, softly kisses with the tongue gentle as a dove.)

He then caresses all the way down slowly to her vaginal and biting gently her inner thigh. They both move to the bed, while 1-female goes and gives thanks with the elixir of ecstatic delight, brings it to the bed and all drink deeply until the chalice is drained.

The whole ceremony in the chamber is brightly lighted in red and there are four big screen televisions with extremely erotic sexual act's playing with lustful Catholic girl's in their church with a perverted Catholic priest. This is to keep the atmosphere in proper sync.)

MALE: For lo, the winter is past and life has come forth. By night I sought my two queens to be by my side. Your beauty shall be with me forever.

Come nigh me...

(The male lay's on the bed with one female on each side holding them close with their legs over his. The females would not let go until erotic ceremony is over.)

MALE: BEHOLD, you are fair my ladies and anything you ask you shall receive of me. We shall now partake of honey and sweet rolls with milk and pleasant fruits.

(While they partake of the offerings Frankincense/Myrrh is lit and they give thanks to all the representations of sex, gods' and goddess'. The male then praises the two females and worship's them and also says.)

MALE: I rejoice for my soul had made me to have in my possession two queen goddess'.

BOTH FEMALE: Our heart has awakened to you! Open for me your heart as ours longs for you.

We sought you and you found out our darkly love.

FEMALE 2: My beloved you have cold eyes of radiance and your mouth is most sweet.

(The music is played by Chopin.)

MALE AND BOTH FEMALES ALL SAY:

And now this ceremony is complete. We are finished.

What A Blessing!

We gather together in unholy fellowship. We come into this place because our hearts seek darkness. For the ways of the wicked are just. We bless thee soldier and defile with curses the rotten mind, for the left hand path we shall follow. We know not the things we do because magic has no limits. Things work out for the best even thou we do not understand ourselves but our God is very close to us. We know not the elements that make up our bodies except what is apparent. For our God knows everything and our God is in ourselves! Shallow minded men spawn together as thy intelligent do also, but thy shallow minded men know not thy reality. It has been said:

"There are not any gods' but for us and we hold reign upon this field. Know that I shall forever be, for my kingdom come and my will be done. It is me who give unto you for all things come accordingly from me. I take from others so that you have a bountiful plenty. You are my true followers and I call you my sons whom I am well pleased."

If you give unto me, then I will and shall give unto thine one-hundred fold. If you take from me then I will destroy you fully. There are nine cycles and nine times purified. We shall be refined like the metal of silver. Eternity awaits us for all mankind has been sentenced to death. We know our end will come in due time as for my God will take over my spirit for eternity. We learn through living, to get rid of our pains and our sorrows, we have to cast all thy impudent cheats away. To learn how to maintain obedience! He wants us to come as we are. I will safe guard by my God as long as I maintain self-control and abide by the law of nature that Govern me.

By all that I know, I trust in my God to deliver me from harm. He will construct me anew, for pure I shall become in all-his kingdom. I have been given the things of the world and I shall know what it is like to have all. I am a model and a leader who has established leadership upon this world and we find true unity among these chosen. Wide is the gate and the souls come dirt cheap in these present nights. Many are throw away that we just don't need and find no use for them. Far greater is he who can create something out of nothing. Listen to what I am saying the great-spirit. Be patient and tolerant for what is to come. This cycle brings fire. There are so many truths that are hidden and you have to find them, their not going to be handed to us. Yes, what I tell you and preach is the truth. There are so many things that go so much deeper than our understanding that's where faith comes in being as believing in ourselves for the matter. Call upon our Dark Lord and he will come to you. The thunders in my hand don't seem to stop, the voices call to me louder as the dead speak to me, for I am one who can see the dead, a gift to me it is. I do hear the calling for my life and the message I will spread, until I am not of any use any longer. This world is full of free spirits but everyone is confused. People don't know what to do or believe any longer. They stumble around in the dark not knowing what they do. Anyone can succeed in Lucifer's work all you have to do is believe in yourself. He will grant us all our indulgences.

Deception is brought forth to lift you up, to rise above to make the fools who are blinded to fall away, it is a tool that is revealed to us and we employ unto others. It is another form of misdirection and can be used at any time.

The greatest gift that has been given to us was knowledge and it came from Lucifer God of Wisdom. He is the churches best and most accompanied friend. We face our fears and into thee eyes of the unknown we share with infernal malice to a holy god for his lies of sanctity. O' impudent Christ we condemn your every way and your very action. DIE you bastard Christ according to the law of Satanic prosperity.

Omnious voritou ala-go-vita lasina matu via noca preastuc miasta!

Covina tuki mastu nini bi sa tu mi otla ma ka to mak nanu vi so kiki.

DOMINUS INFERUS VOBISCUM.
HAIL INFERNAL LORD.
(HOLD SIGN OF CORNUTA UP AND SAY)
OUR GOD IS WITH US!
Ala susu miti vitu suka es maka vi nemasatu bi be ne.

Amen.
Blessed is our dark lord Lucifer of all creation.
Blessed is he who follows the left hand path.
Cursed is he who disobeys.
Blessed is he who delights in Lucifer.
Blessed is he who brings wrath upon the Christian nation.
Blessed is he who lives as the daemons.
Blessed is the unholy fellowship.

Without death there would be no balance. The fires of Hell represent life and desire, I pour out the coals before you. In the same degree our powers shall rise and there would be nothing to stop you. Go the distance and stop at nothing, until you succeed. The dark cloud lives in each of you and it's waiting for your calling. Satanism is a way of life and by living this way you break the chains that bind you. You become a slave to nothing, we worship nothing but ourselves. We believe in ourselves and believing in ourselves is what truly matters. I don't believe in giving hand outs because if a person can not help themselves then why should I help them. These people are just another Vampire of psychic nature. I keep my death close to me as you should to. Do thing's carefully watching your every move. A person can't or I should say a Satanist can not afford to be dumb at all. Rise up saith the Lord Lucifer and we shall become a nation above nation. Know what you do and research it and understand the meaning behind it or else leave it alone. I say awaken my brothers to divulge our enemies and feast upon them because it has become a travesty as they try to destroy a man's dream. We are here to build up the Satanic Empire and calling upon death to awaken.

Hail Satan.

Silver #30

The silver platter symbolizes the end of a path and the beginning of a new. This platter signifies the devil's reign on earth and the Satanist shall stand in power.

Silver is the opposite of gold, just as Hell is opposite of heaven.

Gold has always been connected to heaven, as it shows hypocritical self innocence of a so-called godliness. Silver is the devil's finest, as it has always been used for wicked deeds of man.

Silver in its purest form, holds the greatest of all occult powers, dark forces, and daemonic presences of opposition to heaven.

Silver pieces: an early form of money used in the betrayal of all that is holy and murder to man who claimed divinity above every other god.

Hail to Satan for that...

Silver #30 Part 2

1. Silver was paid, as a lie had built unto itself a throne of pain and suffering.
2. Silver was given as a vote of enforcement for the birds of the air, the fish of water, and earth bound creatures non-human, and to get rid of Jesus the real prince of vile poison.
3. Silver is water.
4. Silver is fire.
5. Silver is air.
6. Silver is earth.
7. Silver is spirit.
8. Silver is sun.
9. Silver is moon.
10. Silver is Pluto.
11. Silver is the life force of outer space.
12. Silver is plant life.
13. Silver is all mankind.
14. Silver is Mars.
15. Silver is Venus.
16. Silver is Uranus.

17. Silver is Saturn.
18. ilver is individuality.
19. Silver is creativity.
20. Silver is lust.
21. Silver is sloth.
22. Silver is gluttony.
23. Silver is anger.
24. Silver is envy.
25. Silver is Jupiter.
26. Silver is pride.
27. Silver is greed.
28. Silver is the law of the jungle.
29. Silver is self-preservation.
30. Silver is all Satanic Victory.

Is What Matter's

I find that the belief in right and wrong will differ greatly between each individual. A person's own standards determine how they live.

For instance, sex offenders see there is nothing wrong with what they are doing. They don't feel they should get punished for hurting women and children.

I believe a law of nature is: If you do something to affect another individual in a way that causes their struggle to live peaceful and content, then you've done something wrong and it's not okay to scare someone for the rest of their lives.

I believe the penalty for such crime should be castration and life imprisonment without parole. These, sex offenders are real scum of the earth.

The subject of drug offenders! In my thoughts, I feel more intense program's and treatment facilities should be brought into existence to help aid the individual in past life problem's. I don't believe that drug's are the main problem on the individual. I believe that drugs are a tool picked up to cover the more serious problem. Drugs and alcohol is just a vehicle to push away past memories, everyday life struggles, and trying to cope with childhood abuse of all forms.

The treatment needed to help addicts and alcoholics overcome is the motivator, the driving force that makes them want to use. If the addict and alcoholic are able to overcome the past and present problems, then they would have no reason to use or drink.

We need more centers brought into existence that help people with hidden problems instead of the open problem.

On the topic of sex offenders they should have to go through a very extensive six year sex offender program and have to pass a very difficult test. I believe frontal lobotomy should be done on all sex offenders if they are not going to get a hard prison sentence.

The Temple Of Sodom

The gathering of wicked spirits, have come forth upon this world. The time had come for a sacrifice to be made.

There were thirteen daemons in a circle. One of them is a high priest. All were wearing black hooded robes with their eyes glowing of the fires of Hell.

Altogether there were nine circles forming an inverted pentagram. In the heart of this was a large fire burning real bright and it was roaring with lost souls. Each circle had a high priest.

On their foreheads was the number three hundred thirty three. The sacrifice was flesh and blood. First, the altar was consecrated in the Dark Lords name; asking the blessing's of Hell upon them and this magical night.

The time had come for the rebirth of Satan to enter into the chosen ones flesh.

The human sacrifice was tied to the ground with arms and legs stretched out. It was tied with black ropes made from hemp. These sacrifices were staked to the ground with stakes nine inches long. On the belly the deacon's dip their fingers in goat blood and write a pentagram. Also, on the forehead was written in the blood six hundred sixty six.

Keep in mind that all nine circles had their own sacrifice, and each sacrifice being a different race. This signifies dominion over the world.

All the sacrifices were sprinkled with incense. At each point of the pentagram was place with the elements: fire, air, earth, water, and spirit. Also, surrounding the whole working were 100 inverted cross'. This is the cross of Peter. This symbolical meaning is the denial of Christ.

In a cave nearby, the most powerful Dark Gods' of the left hand path have risen from Hell and the gates were opened. The sky flashed with lightening one thousand forty nine times and for three hours non-stop it thundered.

In this cave the Dark Gods' were chanting during this whole magical working to raise energy. The high priest in all the circles started to recite to opening invocation, then following the Enochian Call.

The atmosphere came to a complete dead silence. The chosen child for Satan to enter was placed in the middle of the circle, in the cave, where the Dark Gods' were chanting. The daemons in all nine circles started multiple ongoing conjurations for two hours. Each high priest then takes the charged ritual knife and draws blood into the vile of glass from the sacrifice of each race and seals it. The conjurations stop. Each priest picks up a scroll in order 1-9 and each circle had its own number. They were opened in order. A blessing was asked for each sacrifice, one after the other and says: "I ratify and refresh my promise. I honor you in all things. May this sacrifice be a pleasing gift unto you and in your eyes, may it be acceptable. Hail Satan. Long Live The King who enhances himself in all the worldly thing's. The ruler of Hell we greet you as family. Come through thy Baphomet O' Great One and do not make us wait any longer.

Hail to our Ancient Dreams."

The sacrifices were then killed. Then at once the presence entered the chosen one's body. So he began to walk the earth. Satan then speaks: "Forever it is established."

The Adversaries Of Christ

Peter - Was a follower of Jesus for a short time. Peter ended up turning against Jesus and denying him three times before the Jews killed Jesus to avoid his own death. After Jesus was killed the Jews found out about Peter. Because, he had once followed Jesus, the Jews also hated him. The Jews also knew Peter denied Jesus three times before he died to avoid his own death. So, to show his denial of Christ, the Jews crucified Peter upside down on the inverted cross. Now, satanic people take up the symbol and denial of god.

Judas Iscariot - Was also a short time follower of Jesus but had broken free from the lies and deception and the weakness that was being preached. It has been said that Jesus himself caused that to happen by cursing Judas Iscariot his own follower and possessing him with a daemonic entity.

Judas Iscariot sold and gave Jesus up to his enemies for thirty silver pieces. That was the price for a slave.

We champion silver as the adversary to Jesus and heaven.

Cain - An age old warrior and rebellious person against god. His brother Abel loved god, so Cain killed him. Cain hated god with his whole heart, all the way until his death. His body exploded in one of the fields that Abel took care of. That field is now called "The Field of Blood". The book of Cain is very dark and satanic. It was written in his blood and improbable to get your hands on it. It is protected under lasers in a museum.

Mary Magdalin - Was Jesus' girlfriend and committed sexual acts with her including kissing her on the lips in a very intimate way on several occasions! That was forbidden back in that time era. It was possible that she was pregnant by Jesus and baring a child by him. What is very interesting is that Mary Magdalin had constantly been possessed by several daemons, not having any control over herself. So, how does this supposed holy person, said to be the son of god or god himself or sent from heaven, what we know as sky fornication with an unholy possessed person? He himself has been defiled. They were not married and she was not a Christian in anyway. Matter of fact, in that time it was sexually immoral and very ungodly. This according to the Christian belief is against god accordingly.

Joseph and Mary - Jesus' parents were fully human and very poor. They had nothing and were not very popular in any way.

Mary indeed, was a false virgin. She in fact was sleeping with Joseph and he got her pregnant. And so, they wanted to become popular and wanted people to like them. They also wanted to feel like they had a great position in life. They made up the best story in the world that would get them there.

Their claim of a holy spirit came out of the sky in the middle of the night and got her pregnant. But wait a minute! I thought this god is supposed to be light and only works in the light. What a contradiction in the Christian belief. They had everything the world had to offer, especially money and popularity. Mankind is always up for a good story and if it is too good, it will last a long time.

Sodom and Gommorah - a place rejected and hated by their god. Including the people who lived in it, were hated to.

Dreampt Spoken to the Unknown

When we drink blood it represents life, vitality, control, and power. We have our victory in Lucifer. Continuance to the next life as we are transformed into daemon's we shall blaspheme and take down our mortal enemy. We stand in the front line to fight for what's Lucifer's. We are true soldiers. We are the vital existence and our works here on earth shall succeed. People out there spend their lives trying to be somebody else, they have lost their way. Therefore, we follow the left hand path. Our Dark Lord shall sustain us and help us carry on through to the end. The true light shines down on us in pure darkness. We have power and dominion over everything on earth. Do not hurt small children, animals, and women. Instead, raise them up to a singularly extraordinary life of beauty and joy.

Many people do not agree with our way, but they only deny their very reality, they turn to a god who will not save them. They pray and he won't listen, he just turns his head and allows thing's to happen and many times get worse for them. They spend their whole life searching for these spiritual pipe dreams, they will never come true. This world will not change, it will always be. They call upon their god, but he does not hear, but surely my God hears me and he will grant me the things we desire. Be obedient and patient, the time will come. Our God is sheer perfection, don't you believe he can do anything because he is you. Just search your heart and find the true inner self and, you find true happiness and joy, then the rest will come.

Dark Lord, come into our lives and fulfill our desires. We come to you as faithful servants of thy self and we do thy will. Grant us fulfillment of worldly thing's for the world is our heritage, forces of darkness I command you come unto thy throne of thy self and instill within us thy power of wealth through our greatest talents. Blessed be unto thy self, a beast in this field. Grant us this in your behalf O' Great Dark One! Only you know the words I speak and this only request. Knowledge and thy ability for these written words are what I know and shall be granted.